OSTEOMYELITIS

Harry Polkinhorn

Ex Press
San Diego, CA
2014

http://www.harrypolkinhorn.org

Osteomyelitis
is published by Ex Press, San Diego, CA 92122.

ISBN: 13: 978-1500315399

FIRST EDITION PRINTED IN THE

UNITED STATES OF AMERICA

Cover photograph by Cecilia Polkinhorn
madcapvision.com

http://www.harry polkinhorn.org

logo design by Guillermo Nericcio García

by Harry Polkinhorn
(selected)

The River (2012)
Demos Oneiron (2011)
Analysis (2011)
The Circle of Willis (2010)
Trauma (2010)
Bridges of Skin Money (1986, 2008)
Raven (2003)
Tayet's Bandages (1999)
Blue Shift (1999)
Throat Shaadow (1997)
Mount Soledad (1996)
Teraphim (1995)
Anaesthesia (1985)
Travelling with Women (1983)
Volvox (1981)
Radix Zero (1981)

Hematogenous osteomyelitis originates in the metaphysis of tubular long bones adjacent to the epiphyseal growth plate. Thrombosis of the low-velocity sinusoidal vessels from trauma or embolization is considered the focus for bacterial seeding in this process. This avascular environment allows invading organisms to proliferate while avoiding the influx of phagocytes, the presence of serum antibody and complement, the interaction with tissue macrophages, and other host defense mechanisms. The proliferation of organisms, the release of organism enzymes and byproducts, and the fixed-volume environment contribute to progressive bone necrosis.

Netter's Infectious Diseases, 2012, p. 214

OSTEOMYELITIS

I Hematogenous Infection from Bacteremia

1
How to deploy, among the wonderful confusion of a lifetime's detritus, big weapons, big because of their seeming insignificance, flops itself right out here and demands my full attention. Notice which edges of the leaf are sharp as glass broken in a rage. Every day there is a vast renewal, even as a layering in memory thickens. I read today that the chances of a huge earthquake here in the next 30 years are 99%.

2
Once the decision has been made, it's only now a question of time. Then we'll see another side of things, where the blowhole releases its contents again and again, and I stand by awestruck, or is it an inability to comprehend? Night comes on with a soft fury, setting up the war in my brain like opposing chess pieces of both sexes armed with the latest in military hardware.

3
I remember, and in the act draw a line that launches ships, asserts the radical imagination that will lead to the kingdom of shadows. Less is required, yet for that gain I have to agree to a payment schedule brutal in its simplicity and grace. Just being able to speak, and speaking, causes the sun to reappear, having been recalled from its grave in the miracle of irrelevant calendars, castrated chronicles of the sad doings of people crawling or racing through their days.

4
Now comes the pain as she prepares to leave, casting me back into a world of the half-living. But who sets down these cold

numbers, when my job is to battle their obligatory assaults? Nothing has changed in decades—the shame and rage get purer over time, stretching me out thin as hammered brass. Let's assume the least and pack up dead relatives now that Christianity has run its course. An airy good-bye sparks an avalanche, and renegades stab me in the heart over and over.

5
The four walls lock me down into a vision of imperfection, an artificial paradise that resists incursions. Instead, I tally wins and losses, careful to include all the furniture of a stripped mind. Fat women shriek downstairs, dead-set on confirming a harsh illness, this one all too contagious. Gradually, I settle down. Late afternoon bleeds into evening again. Reassurances are tendered and rejected.

6
Reconfiguring turns out to be more complicated. Simple desire must give way to things of a cold beauty. I abide by these provisional truths, thirsty for the right words that will shut down circuitry. Ink smears replace living language as it forges ahead blindly, taking me to its own destination.

7
In the very sinuosity of these vines, deep troughs dug out by age, I place myself lovingly because of the black juncture. Sometimes I'm face down with an eye to the past, harrowing compact sludge in the core drillings of memory. Notably, people have vanished. A patch of snow under trees outside of Madrid, or the steady silent throb of the Arno matches the maps I pored over as a child, trying to imagine the real thing somewhere else, anywhere else. Now through a looping I['m planted in myself like a stake through the gut.

8
The morning weeps from a wounded sky necrotic with gray. I am helped slowly into my mind's casket, prepared for the journey they sing about. Long ago I said my good-byes, beaten out of me

with leather belts and coat hangers. But there's no neutral ground where the hole can be dug.

9
What would work when work itself falls under suspicion, seen as the activity of a manipulator? I swallow a mouthful of dirt and dead leaves. The exact quality of light has become impervious to all human construction, so my respectful attention is shrugged off. Note to myself: even though you have to, don't put up with it any more. Just because you are alive doesn't mean you have to go on living.

10
Vanity in the texture of a doomed afternoon, marked out for certain destruction. Vanity and ignorance slowly accumulate even as meaning drains out drop by drop, like parenteral poisons leaking into channels. The hummingbird sews its pattern because it has to, and I return my mind to the green and gray, so patient but nevertheless always moving and changing. That much I've learned despite my misplaced humility.

11
A bubbling, swelling surface conducts you towards possible hyperplasia, as if your knowledge could ward off the random shufflings. In these haunts a different law rules, according to which cascades are fixed. That much is certain. Fluid dynamics expose the inner workings, and each intelligence serves only one master. I see this and wonder about the things I can never know, as you do or will in time. Way back when I strayed from their track, still occasionally visible in the middle distance but not directly underfoot. In exchange I find mildness and acceptance in this antechamber, or have I crossed a threshold that changes everything?

12
The world's huge rickety contraption lurches along, and I feel the blood begin to pool. Cautious creatures extend their senses against an unforgiving wall, an impenetrable thicket coated with

cold rain. To drift elsewhere invites attack. I cannot allow myself to forget the war in Afghanistan or smooth lies in Washington, D.C. They, too, commandeer the common tongue and cast it into hollow-points to do maximum damage.

13
Who controls the flow of particles charged to repel invaders or the merely curious? Craft and a capacity to wait them out come to my aid as I contract, assuming a coiled posture. These are lean seasons, my inability to grasp the guy wire fully exposed. Just because I've been opposed doesn't automatically lead to such dire conclusions, although trends have a magnetic pull. I observe my surroundings, as usual, and reel in my mind from its incessant wanderings. Hugely emotional events go out over the airwaves, cutting up our lives into bite-sized chunks.

14
I'm drying out on these shores after the shipwreck. Dazed, I look around, not used to such harsh light. Salt scales cover my skin, and only after some adjustment will I be able to pull together a sequence of memories, images troubling the interface. One is my father at 93 showing me accounting sheets he has filled out in pencil tracking every penny. I realize I'm now in the future although not really, because these are just words, random digits spun out to stave off solitude, thereby creating it.

15
Who wants to know about such matters? Avoidance at all costs since to do otherwise courts a corrosive criticism. Yet I can't help myself, not even able to imagine who might eventually enter these parts. I suppose the ritual must run its predictable course, or my shaky sense would be further jeopardized. But what about the great diaspora, sad leave-taking because the Red Army is advancing? I pick up an awl and punch leather with the symbols my hands have memorized.

16
The ravages of love have left me, no longer a willing votary of wishing. Cannibals appear around the periphery, armed to the teeth. Waves of fear tear me down, while the neighbors are having drinks or celebrating someone's birthday. How long has it been? Years. The same old comments sicken me.

17
What I was never allowed to say comes back in dreams and a profound unease: when will the next blow fall? A pattern of petechia points to internal disharmony, a scrambling of sequences that keep firing away but not as originally laid out. I feel this and note that the hallway mirrors have been draped in black. Faux Corinthian columns line a broad drive. Cars arrive and depart with a discrete stately hush as dignitaries come to pay respects, staged but somehow necessary, at least in their view.

18
Not just any form pulled from the air will do. A constant sifting and sorting fashions qualities of longing, a base beat of hatred for what they did. Now the world pulls down its steel shutters. You train yourself not to hear the howling, or if you can't at least not to be disturbed unduly.

19
They left just enough for me to crawl into a nearby cave or declivity in the woods. Any chance of being evocative of care was almost surgically removed, their methods so unwittingly thorough. Yet I can still feel my feet as I make my slow way down, dragging along behind me. There are no people here, nor will there ever be. I'm acutely aware of my situation, and it makes no difference that I don't like it. I hear the whirring of power drills as they screw down the lid. At some point the cold and dark become my medium.

20
Polite conversation avoids such matters. A parade or cortege vies mightily with mundane coffee cups and ticket stubs, crews laying

asphalt, the mournful dirge of anonymous engineers and their dreamy-eyed assistants pausing for a smoke. Blustery winds rip apart and reassemble chunky clouds. Who gives a shit? The spider disappears into its stony waiting.

21
I go back to the well because not to do so would hasten an erosion, a sterilizing of these fruits. Don't expect an impossible clarity, lucid dreams you can feel happy controlling. Each step costs more than the last, and no one has to tell me what to do. A blind craving powers those constructions, which then become saturated with moisture and fully primed and seeded. Who would guess? Intense disappointment grows into a tearful rage and then exhaustion. You look on from your safe, sealed distance, and no wonder.

22
I had to tender my resignation, despite an influx of manufactured sunlight and bonhomie. Across a canyon the silent processes of nature grind on. Excess liquids bleed off, reestablishing an electrolytic balance. Gradually, the angularities of the city take shape, before dissolving back into the gloom. Under such conditions I can't distinguish parameters, much less a particular plan at work. Instead, hours go by while I pretend, now that the old schemes and plots have lost their pull. My frank reflection on the tyranny of daily life just contributes to a carnival atmosphere. Polyps proliferate. Certainties about the building code or approved safety procedures rankle in the soul because how can they compete with the movement of water? Tiny fragments speed through the ether. As such, a general reduction is called for.

23
The carousel spins, sending out pennants and shredded calliope notes, but in the end coal dust and road grime win out. However, a check of the rhythm reveals what I suspected, namely, a long arc. Independent assessment yields vague statements about

mortality or the molecular basis of the various Coxsackie virus subtypes. How could it be otherwise?

24
They said it was coming, and here it is. I'm strapped down for the duration, and even at that the outcome remains doubtful. Musclemen are hooked up to monitors, televisions yammering away. All I can do is hunker down to protect myself from the blows. Personal preferences among to jack, but they cannot be discounted. You see a pattern and think it could be a way out, but don't be hasty. What I imagined as miraculous takes on a different quality under the stark illumination of money and power.

25
Where are the edges? An exploration carries me right up to a black gas. It seems best to take stock before proceeding, but a shroud covers the sacred object, one way or the other. Ownership guarantees nothing. You sometimes lie awake at night, listening for marauders. The safety is off, the chamber loaded. Any thought of love or easy conversation almost stuns you with its irrelevance because 100% of your mind must point towards true north. The reckoning of accounts can come later, if at all. My simple requests go unheeded since in so many ways I don't exist. The weaving ensnares me as I realize it's my only chance, to survive through dying, which bears my remains across the divide. I press my wrist and thigh to verify further possibility but can't go it alone. Yet I'm alone.

26
Where again? Quid pro quo, or rough justice. I must absorb influx, because they say so. Beneath the layers of chattering and rushing, I'm immersed in a river of lava, the pyroclastic flow that destroys everything in its path, including the path. That's why each departure must somehow stay true and define its own particular itinerary, maybe the great pyramid or Death Valley through the warm glass of a Le Sabre window. But no. Protuberances and discolorations arise and disappear from my

skin like clouds. I notice the activity although without comprehension. It's a simple enough statement.

27
There wasn't enough, and their random coming and going couldn't be systematized, punctuated as it was by mockery and slaps. Cycles of wishing and despair laid trenches for cabling and pipes. Eventually, any evaluation had to become cursory, and of course it did. I couldn't use my signaling array. Trigger circuits were fashioned and installed. Getting from here to there, fingers fumbling in the dark to trace and memorize my own face, an outline nameless and apart slips into place.

28
There it is again. The corruption of human nature soaks into the soil underfoot, a collusion I cannot escape. Invoices will be provided on request. I told you at the outset, so don't get all huffy. The blind, deaf, and lame go for broke, pitifully. Somehow I know these things, yet my very limited capacity plays out despite having been hedged in with provisos and qualifiers, clever disguises, Venetian masks. Why wasn't my opinion sought?

29
To vanquish the enemy—simply consult a manual. Retracting the document lies outside the purview. I shuffle the deck, taking in a quotient of air and light, since osmotic exchange characterizes life itself. Let's see that these instruments say, now that my repairman has done and gone. I've relinquished what little control I had, and look at the ever-loving consequences. Incredible.

30
I ask myself what the actual loss would come to, and no ready answer appears. From this the step to death or panic is too abrupt. She waits in the wings for her chance to shine. Guards form up into orderly ranks, and thin militia oil their weapons. All it takes is one accurate load to accomplish that task. I'm crawling along under a dense layer of smoke, fighting for each breath.

Something in me refuses to accept what my senses are telling me. Whispers from the supposed beyond get shredded by the sounds of massive explosions that cause the ground to shake. When I start to realize my role, it's too much.

31
Boss man cracks his whip, and the dogs cower. Any beauty along the river's green edge retreats. I remember my childhood in the desert, its oppressive hot winds laden with choking dirt, or the stifling humidity and stench of cow shit from feed yards. An acidic slime coats my throat. Cholesterol winks through the fog as I flee, barely able to register the wild barking from across town. How the night air carries that angry, incessant protest. It goes on and on in my mind for decades. I draw a finger through dust that covers the walls and furniture. A centipede coordinates its movement, leading inevitably down through cracks in the floorboards. I notice everything, and none of it has meaning. The house, built in 1915, is collapsing. They should never have come here in the first place but were driven by their restless tortured spirits. Now it's up to me.

32
Why so quiet? The utter regularity of my days might suggest otherwise, but not so fast. The Star of David or secret insignias prepare another way every bit as legitimate, and yet your tendency is to negate as long as pharmaceuticals keep on flowing. But then you wonder, having become landlocked due to their incursions. Doors close as liquids run downhill if the tubes have been well situated. Each piece matters; you can feel it. No blame. I pick up the burden, bitter yet somehow glad for this chance. I hope my credentials are in order because the gold has eluded me.

33
Songs burn to ash in my mouth. Despicable behavior initiates a round of ugliness and fury. Animal control won't help; I'm on my own. I've heard their stories and excuses while submitting to irrational demands. No more. From here on out it will be stones, sand, and cultural trash.

34
Medical school extends their reach since the honchos have it planned out. What, in fact, goes unsaid? I decide to up my game although their half-baked opinions will still have to be dismissed. Liar. Come back from the pit and face your accusers. The hour-glass can only be reversed or shattered. Nazis or Mafia, take your pick because with the setting sun a new world order hatches out. Strait jackets are heaped up for burning, at last. Images materialize before me, which I confuse with other images, and the terror squads infiltrate government agencies, schools, and hospitals. News accounts undergo careful pre-screening. What used to be private drips or gushes into pipelines, and the dismal whorehouses of bygone eras are resurrected in another form.

35
You will have noticed anxious dreams, a view of the past unrealistic yet persuasive, suppressed trembling. I, too, have been imprinted, and must learn to accept in the broadest sense. Kiss-asses forge on ahead, creating a vacuum soon to be filled with the sad cast-offs of a disturbed society. Despite what I see, speed settings remain unchanged until a fresh apocalypse is upon us, at which point any further talk becomes academic, that is, unhinged. Bronchitis or telangiectasis rules the roost.

36
Terrible loneliness returns like evening fog, making all but itself invisible, or at least blunting my responses. What cycle of destruction and renewal will come to replace the effusions of a generous world gone haywire? Who has that kind of patience? My claim has shrunk to an allotment of air, and how light modulates; there is no harm in noticing. Says who? Offloading dead weight sets the contraption in motion with its attendant maudlin blathering over grandchildren, who could care less.

37
A helicopter roars by lest I forget. Skilled fingers reset controls to their null positions, where shadows pool along floorboards or underneath the fountain bowl. I'm tuned to the proper tensions,

but little remains, just occasional mild breezes, the weak panting of a dying afternoon. As if on cue, explosives experts and snipers start showing up in the briefing room. After all, only by disconnecting the router will I be able to carve out a niche. Always pay cash. That way when they come to scare the weaker creatures, it will seem as if parasites might evade their own categorical imperative: multiply or die. Yet things are rarely that black or white. If you don't make the cut, there is a separate pathway.

38
Precious little. Don't worry. Without your daily regimen, the house of cards crumbles. Loud noises mark that passing, as I tally losses because the exact pattern of scars seals my fate. The crows keep it up, even before dawn. Their optimistic music welcomes the first softening grays. These matter. Edema stirs the pot, along with various opaque coefficients, until you wake up screaming. Something has gone seriously afoul, and righting the ship violates ethical principles. Precise miniature armatures transmit dynamic ideas across time and space. All digital, but even that is insufficient.

39
A profile makes its statement with Attic clarity, yet I retract my feelers and press on over the endless dunes. My paltry attempts to reconstruct their practices in another medium yield complicated reflections. Instead, the blandishments of a tropical isle dull the instrument. Another knowledge holds sway, and deepening reveals its hunger despite all that has happened since. A viscous light oozes over the horizon. The implicate order rejects bashing, which is as it should be. Breakers roll on majestically, and although all this will end I won't see it because resources are limited, the usual case.

40
Or? Clinical pearls won't cover the field. Stem cells deaden sound until better equipment arrives, and it will. Back up out of the dreck. Mere maintenance doesn't do it. How do you calculate that

value if fear swamps your mind? Nowhere else can cilia in such numbers be found. Attack and defense jockey for position. I thrash around, no time to feel ashamed.

41
Unremarkable, I trudge on, taking readings from time to time. At last the illness relents. Trapped in circumstance, I hatch it forth while holding my breath. Stereoscopic vision and opposable thumbs sing their threnody, and I hurry along with my task.

42
My cheeks flush. Together, we labor up the mountain, but the settings, although automatic, are all screwed up. The unearthing continues, and pneumatic drills get with it. I've absorbed my limit. Slight deviations produce huge consequences. The skin has its own reasons, if you can call them that. None of this adds up, but large pressures to continue are undeniable, and ultimately the slow grinding together of tectonic plates deep in the gut wears me down. I hear snatches of an old-fashioned waltz and long painfully for anything beautiful in the midst of this nightmare.

43
Whether stuck or moving, I'm thrust over a threshold. Smoke rises, then descends, and my gratitude runs out. Someone else, equally nameless, hefts an axe. My daily ration is dished out callously because it's always that way, so why would I expect anything different?" A choice is made, and the loneliness of cut flowers in a vase is devastating. I'm felled like an ox with a round to its brain. My old heart can't do it any more. Nevertheless, an obduracy insists on its own version, grand or petty notwithstanding. I clear my throat again and speak out but to what end when the groaning spirits flock and flutter to the cleft? There is no dress code down here. Stimulants must be replenished before we are allowed to partake. Receive the papal blessing, and proceed to the consistory. All those neglected desires keep on cresting.

44
One is allowed a fixed amount. I learned this early on, although without understanding. Anonymous agents appear at the door, and the national stinginess crystallizes before my eyes. You may feel impelled to question, but I would think twice before launching a campaign. Consultation or lies. Their irrefutable logic stumbles on its own grace and clarity. Will I finish before the place caves in? Don't count on it. Immobility precedes contraction. One by one they succumb, and sheer numbers guarantee nothing more than a reassuring illusion.

45
I pull back from that prospect, almost in shock. A child's mind teems. Hours pass, and I look blankly in the multiple mirrors, because the house is empty, a repository of dead echoes.

46
Later, a shifting of exotic plants, chain link, chrome alloys, and apartment complexes produces its share of cellular pathways, the epiphenomena caught up in nets of words and calculus. Chariots bake in midday heat. Why am I? There is no other way to read it. Hundreds of pages blow down city streets, the hard despair of wasted lives visibly inscribed. These epistles prey upon the unwitting. Framed, I cynically swallow, since watchful visages plan their next move with aplomb or a diplomatic frisson. That's just how it goes. Nothing personal.

47
When the proverbial hammer falls, I'm ready. I'm rested and in attack mode, so that my effusions of pain can be contained. The smell of sulfur mixes with ammonia and engine grease. Options are foreclosed. Pressure points chart an order purely of the mind's own making, fabulous creatures in the night sky. I seek refuge among busted sofa springs, chunks of concrete, glass shards, tiny markings on random surfaces that commemorate someone's protest or unexplained resignation. You hear what you can, and the rest goes by, while my face burns with consequences. Another cycle completes itself.

48
As if held in abeyance, I repeat a construction of plants, early love, the powerfully surging river seen by moonlight. All arrive and take their assigned places. You figure it out, then strike the appropriate pose, which works. Must I again review my charts? At zero setting. I'm begging for I know not what, but the raw acceptance of insults and mockery demands an apology I can't or won't give. A scalpel of insight releases blood and philosophy. Swarms of connections begin to flicker and fade. Up the output. I envision a movie star entering a hotel that has been converted into a church or cult headquarters. Storms of cells trouble the matrix, and the trips get longer the less I love.

49
On the forefront or back burner, I rally my waning forces for one more assault. The simplest description punishes evolution, but in the end who cares? Where will I be? Getting through another hour seems monumental. Then comes an onrush. The forgiveness of sins. Hurry up and wait for some fantasy, which by its mandate cannot be other. You could enter denominations in your record books, but when the money stagnates minimal alterations appear. Obsidian eyes glint. I am the robot, clanking through my portion. Bring on your vacuum seals, your electronically controlled locks, whatever human ingenuity can devise. A bold phallic push carries them to their destiny or progeny. Basalt blocks obstruct your tender passage.

50
The pain signals my distress, and I have mistaken love for shielding from fear, so that work must be performed now, like it or not. The path twists and turns back on itself, like oxen in a field, going forward by going backward. What have you accomplished today? Rushing footsteps spur me on as though hexed by the biological trap. No room at the inn. I feel a chill break on my neck, a crackling of porcelain. Someone will call, but I won't answer. At last dim comprehension begins after the sickness. Obscure, all but forgotten thinkers can provide little; I'm certain of it. Needles tremble but give readings, and the show

goes on. My objections thin out in recognition of this new condition, the elevation they coveted and now possess.

51
I'm deeply humiliated but not completely dead. The synergy between such petty concerns and a purported national interest stuns the general population, but you just tune it out blithely with another round of evening newscasts. An original mind takes a stab. My obsessive counting and recounting cannot stay the execution. We enter a shadowy glen, moving along under giant oaks. Others have been here before because of the track and broken stalks. Predestination goes the way of all flesh, hitting a plateau at noon when a down phase kicks into gear. Defeat feels familiar, and I stand before gathered senators to argue my case. You assemble your troops, having subjected them to arbitrary commands, and they comply but must be watched under gunpoint. Disembodied voices nag and plague you, to which you can't help but listen, searching for clues and patterns.

52
Partial cumulative trauma produces hairline fractures, downgrading my load-bearing capacity. Now you know, so shut up. Factor in their particular advantages, making sure to rub them down. While waiting, I balance the books because caution is your watchword.

53
A tattered nylon flag hangs listlessly from its rope. Who knows where we are, really? Someone assigned conventional classifications, figuring that was it, but was it? Not that long ago I wouldn't have been able to sit here. The bones of the dead have turned to dust, delivering the ultimate one-two punch. My hair is gone. Next will be my teeth and eyes. What could be more comical? Pools of dried vomit form a path that leads out, but their complicity underlies any contractual concessions. I know it sounds complicated. The alpha dog will not be mistaken, so I reassess. My stock dwindles by the minute, and that's the point. You rise up in protest, then collapse due to an episode. It's

orthostatic hypotension, nothing more. Guilt seeps through like a noxious gas. The smell of cheap alcohol ruins their plans. What a let-down! Chump change on the counter, and don't play the fool. Half-mast won't do. We're zipping along full throttle. What could be more reassuringly conventional? Ducts are working overtime.

54
Each move snaps into place, and my fear exerts its magnetic pull. You express your care indirectly because how else? I would incinerate the very metaphors before they hit the ground running, as a gold-plated second had sweeps the dial with a majestic indifference. Air catches in my throat. Who are these hardened mercenaries dressed in gray-green uniforms that blend into the background? Such longing for you, to take away my panic as evening approaches, but you won't or can't. I hold my breath in shallow lungs and bumble on, snared between these walls of my own fabrication. My mind cannot escape despite repeated attempts to scale escarpments. I'm crawling through meat scraps and rusted engine parts. Any slight sound could alert the opposition, which never sleeps. You slowly release bits of information I can use and make my own.

55
I point out the crudely fashioned explosive device to the police chief, who seems to make a mental note. You are nowhere to be found, so I hold off. This isn't a video game. The skill of the ancient hunter comes into play, just more bacterial warfare. They're guarding the copyright or trademark, but I specialize in loss qualities, never thinking twice. Despondent. Biblical patriarchs stride the sands, staff in gnarly hand and surrounded by offspring, which adds its touch. Fungi dig in, assaulting the barrier, feeling for advantage. Get the point? One never knows, easily forgetting between times. Yet look how far it can go. Promises of a better future exert their delusional influence through television or mere word of mouth, and they fall in line. Everyone has to start at the bottom.

56
Pain waxes and wanes with the moon. I'm skimming a surface like a water spider or downhill ski buff. Ratcheting up doesn't matter because the refuse will still have to be burned. Surely you can see this despite guilt, despite lifelong bitter recrimination. A gathering storm precludes customary procrastination, as I dole them out or watch what once seemed so invaluable trickle away. The game rules shift and shift again, but don't allow any breaches because who can see that far? Not I. Pregnancy does the trick as though something could be made up by complying with code. Virtual reality goes in one more meat-grinder. I'm lashed to the main mast and praying for my life, but things don't look good. A middy stroll through the Tuileries, for example, would result in a coughing fit while listening, again, to jets going through their interminable paranoid routines.

57
I doze, waking with a startle. My various tokens have been played, and if I can't accept my lot then I'll plummet anyway. I'm at the bottom of the sea, looking up at waves overhead sweeping along. Growths appear, ugly, hard. Fissures open, from which steam escapes. The line is dead, or dying. The degree of my grandiosity is crushing, unmatched in the annals. Creatures in black suits show up with their clipboards and stopwatches.

58
What are you trying to tell me with your carefully measured words? A cold hand reaches out that cannot be called a bully, and my mind fails. Revelers take to the streets and byways, sending up a din. Meanwhile, scaling goes on unabated, as if the story line didn't merit a goddamn response. Neophytes beware. Slim latitude is granted. Coffee taste lingers, while bizarre characters confirm the general destruction. I heft my weapon, looking through a slot at what may be likely targets. Pinched looks hang in memory. A mesmerizing inner screen displays goods indiscriminately, yet you feel you must go on seeking approval. No doubt.

59
They've moved the firing range. If you stop moving long enough, they'll belie their own positions. Cold-blooded. Fames engulf their treasured holdings. You want free access so you can feel important, further from the actual black gate. A hollow dent collects random particles, laying out a star chart. That's how far it reaches if you get out of the way, but that is a big if. Corpuscles and capillaries ramify and multiply, inviting hostility, but I'm on to their wiles. Minor delight arises from a set of circumstances superior to previously held records, and so on and so forth. Stalkers find it easy to know. Saints and martyrs be damned! To mast their language I had to pout in some serious time. Repetitive sounds stand in for human presence, but there you are. Always going for the red line bankrupts an already shaky system. Whoever violates these precepts can expect like treatment, regardless of personal connections.

60
The level falls. Mercury spreads its contamination with aplomb. What would you check off your list? Sadomasochists abound, alas. Whose solicitation matters more in these barren seasons?

61
Somewhere else the smokers gather now that impulsive follow-up has come to matter so little. Then the real ones vanish over a receding horizon. Western ways spy for those shadowy operations, and I'm left to struggle with paranoia. Soon it's gone. Car engines and footsteps. Savings? You bet! Just follow the rules, but what if they keep changing? Keep following.

62
I retreat, a strategic withdrawal into shades and texture. All but breathless, the vine-covered palm stands just as it always has, then moves slightly with subtle breezes. A door opens, shuts. My concentration on back-up files guarantees nothing, because what I'm building first must reveal its own rhythm. After these pitiful games are concluded, by fiat, I expect heavy equipment, PCV piping, works in protective clothing with safety goggles.

Hypocrites in regalia promulgate their dogma, their disguised gobbledygook. Lines and cubes spread across our constructed playgrounds as columns of ants make their peace in an imperfect world. How many years has it been now since the gravestone was lifted" I go down a staircase to my storehouse. Vast and troubling cloud formations rotate in the neutral sky, sending the populace fleeing, but where to? Dust storms from Chinese deserts choke cities to their knees, and mothers cover their children's faces with rags. You ask yourself quite rightly how the virus broke through, as if to grasp first causes would finally lay that theological ghost.

63
Total immersion launches its campaign of hype. Net gain trumps the encroaching gloom but only as a phase. I haul my sights around, backed up by artillery and air. St. Peter's comes crashing down, another victim of retinopathy, the angiotensin cascade, and these aren't just big words. Get others to pay; that's the narcissistic ticket. Soon a slew of deal-breakers destroy my chances, and tears flow freely, washing away the dead. People assemble lawfully to perform their rituals. Those who are left realize something vaguely disturbing about the pharynx or tachycardia, how the machinery repairs itself despite repeated blows. It's not exactly a sponge. Up bubbles a rookery. The male hormone is synthesized and released because staining action goes unchecked. The neuromuscular junction fails. They turn away in bitter resignation, and you box up your cosmetics for the next leg.

64
Accolades pour in from around the globe, but they cannot stem the sadness. Delicious uncertainties stoke the boiler, oiling an interior mechanism visible only through broncho-alveolar lavage. The horror and screaming fade in time. There can be no gold standard, so you fell yourself another version of the same old story but this one without a single frill. Each drop is squeezed out. Theatergoers demand their money's worth or thereabouts, and things tend not to work out as planned. The young clump,

hoping against hope. I take my case and go home, glad to still have one. These stem cells lines reach out instead of hitting steady state, a lingering whether proximal or distal.

65
Entire battalions are mowed down impartially beneath the scythe, and new waves of centurions form up for the love feast. I look at myself in a mirror shaped like a book. Secret thrills shiver, and vanities burst upon the unsuspecting with the full force of historical inevitability, but what then? Another full moon explains squat. It rages on, until the bell tolls. Pollutants keep an eye out, using all the means at their disposal, but what's the point if Congress lacks the wherewithal? Furthermore, travesties are committed every day, and no one makes a peep. I stumble upon their clues, moving quickly along a miserable option. Return rates are no better and in fact may not be conducive, so hitch up. Passwords are carefully archived under their corresponding categories, appropriate to this situation like an old maxim.

66
Mexicans can, for sure. That's when you really start to get angry. The bellwether masticates with maddening patience while Rome burns in the middle distance. Where is an angel? I cling to my raft and hope for the best in a dire situation. Looking straight into the sun will take care of that. It must be reassuring to imagine you know what's what. Otherwise? Trysts at dusk under a pecan tree, or a mottled sky that fees an apocalyptic imagination confirms some idea like a fuse or trigger safety.

67
I settle back into my trench. Sputum and radiographic studies match wits in a world of gray misery. Don't you get it now? They destroyed the i.d. cards. Fatigue and diarrhea.

68
Filtering never ceases. I steal a few furtive moments here and there, putting together a fake life to get by until my sentence is announced. Age alone saves me, if saving it can be called. A

forsaking trails along behind by only a notch. Everything is available always everywhere. Faces drain empty in a flash, and the wheels cannot be stopped. Ghostly presences lurk behind an arras, fangs bared. Slime coats pipes. Untrammeled intercourse appears briefly on the shimmering horizon, but look. Presto! It's gone. Stylized and stamped deep into meat, my assertion takes a stand, fully knowing something dark and foreboding. Barking stabs the foolish serenity. I'm blamed as a matter of course, a heavy shower of withering abuse. The drumbeats of war go out over the land, and mothers are sobbing in the night. I cultivate my plot, a furrow, wound, or grave, because of an inescapable mandate. My ongoing failure underscores that pain, keeping it alive in my mind. You can spot them a mile off, right? The broken ones, cast aside by torrents of cash, hang their heads like thrashed dogs. A portal to the underworld skulks among you. Hatred boils over, and the untouchables facilitate another revolution. I never made it. My sails are coming down, as deceptive waters flatten out, inviting a reflective trance.

69

Now it all makes sense. That is, how can I hate someone I depend on? There is no distinction between the feeling and its expression. Jets pass overhead, and frogmen fiddle with their equipment. My mind casts about fruitlessly. I butt into their shenanigans.

70

The smell of fresh garbage is stultifying, along with creosote and standing water, reminding me of an alternate reality. I place the objects at our feet, step aside, and wait because at some point a circuit will be closed. That's it. Buxtehude drifts across a hushed auditorium, and spring arrives as if for the first and only time. My neighbor drives off to work, terrified of the stock market, and I applaud. My crucial knowledge of skin and grass, dreams and old doorways, falls into desuetude, while idle threats change into fixed action potentials and fully functioning calcium channels. Do you imagine an ion is insignificant? I place a hand elsewhere temporarily, then take a breath and move on.

71
A friend becomes a grandfather, just like that. The hugeness of an incomprehensible act dwarfs its entire proximity without even trying, jumping through the traditional hoops with unsurprising alacrity. Rarely do these cruel magistrates extend a hand. Effects are generated by virtue of an inferred principle, and once again I'm transported into a field that becomes simultaneously a source of reassurance and fear. We get off the bus, cross an avenue, and gaze out to sea. Mazatlan, 2003. Bruised forearms provide evidence, because traces are left despite concocted stories about being accosted, no to mention mugged. Now it's your turn; I'm pulling back in anticipation.

72
It almost doesn't matter what we discuss as long as crushing pain and sadness appear. Pay what you owe, or they cut off service. Mechanically installed valves and switch boxes direct traffic until the system bends. Acorns pile up. A hot wind disturbs the dead leaves and foxtails, yellow and dry, as though mystical comprehension could mirror that sky show or unpredictably interacting rivulets during a cloudburst. This product really does sell itself. Rusty faucets trouble their visions as the sound of an engine unexpectedly announces their imminent arrival. No more sleeping at the wheel. The walls creak and groan, living things. Discharge your various obligations, no matter how petty, and soon enough other forms of revenge will occur. Mavericks and renegades rush for the doors, always desirous, never satiated.

73
But maybe the insights of today will again turn out to become superseded in another turn of the spiral. Fluids gurgle along merrily, unaware and glad of it. I check for signs. Myalgia punctures that little illusion, and its contents bleed out into language. You have created that which you most feared because of the iron law. Not enough oxygen is getting through, so what do you expect? Shuttling eventually extends the story or texture, but whose vital organs have gone up for sale lately? It's a keeper. Pure speculation, I'd say. Spontaneous generosity goes

unrewarded, as warning signals do their humble jobs. Soon enough you'll find your account tapped, because an external enemy never fails to materialize.

74
They've noticed smaller and smaller amounts and said little or nothing but rolled with the ship. My circle shrinks at a rate beyond perception, which entails dosing with unfractionated heparin, for example. After building in an overview, I decide to excavate a major chamber, the project of years. It's upside down; I know. Defenses and apologia get rid of all opposition. My breathing is steady, with no rales. The machine purrs along, running its diagnostics in the so-called background. Soon the Lord will rise again, and we can excuse irregularities, log jams, abscesses that refuse t heal. Core strength gains your confidence as if sodium excretion bore no responsibility. I reach for my gaff, my hay hooks. Reflex action kicks in, a kind of antiseptic that overrides my constant pain. At this elevation I find my observation unreliable even if other instrumentation is null and void. Steamrollered by evolution, I crawl out, clawing my way along.

75
Executions proceed, until corpses become a problem. Cheating adds spice but can spoil the soup. They're on the look-out, staring into a dark hole for days on end. Fission or fusion, business transactions, drive-by shootings, and normal fluctuations feed their data willingly. We're in this together. To be a man in those ways became unacceptable and impossible. Cold justification replaces heir white bones, and I'm left holding another bag. What do I want, beyond what I already have? The cenotaphs have been knocked over. Heroes can't effect a cure. Snakes, dogs, horses, their chthonic direction exerts an irresistible pull, and you belatedly realize it's long since happened. The poison conceals its antidote, so we have to forge on, like it or not. Somewhere in the woods I find a staff, which I use as a club. My body feeds on itself. Cachexis.

76
Yes, we are far from home. After dark the ascesis lets up long enough for me to hack through bamboo, but I know I'm on borrowed time. Why talk about what isn't here unless it's to build a false monument? What I see won't be arrested, much less hypnotized. Yet a provisional accusation of murder goes a long way. I felt and feel a profound satisfaction when I pulled the plug, getting my retaliation in the end. Nothing is random. Jokes better be good, or grilling will be the least of your worries. Fear-mongers take a number and step aside. I'm moving both towards and away from. How foolhardy have I been? Take a router to it. First do no harm, because full disclosure won't protect you in any event. Who can know what's required when small-arms fire rides rough-shod? Repeating nostrums puts them effectively to sleep. So much unalloyed misery could have been avoided, but let's be frank. Both avenues are closed, and any further requests must be shelved. Boredom won't get you off that hook, so fire up your engine.

77
I can recall a few scraps, an old woman blind in one eye. Tetralogy of Fallot takes over as waves of children and grandchildren crest and break. In fact, little moves. Old flesh runs its course. Multiple insults, fantasy pulls strings. Don't impede free circulation. Fungal colonies spring up overnight, as the ancient war grinds on.

78
What now, another body blow or cornerstone? Mapping procedures were standardized and haven't changed since the Saracens. I wrangle with pillagers, liars, and cheats, yet suicide bombers have nothing of value to lose. Roots bore through. Hogs for fame and money litter a damaged landscape. Contagion-bearing fog creeps up the canyons, advancing its cause, when I notice your waning force field, a disaster in the making. What used to seem automatic has become a weird memory marking off a sacred circle, but the funerals cone on apace. Dancing past

midnight holds the line so that you can sleep. One by one they dip into my black pool.

79
At the crossroads someone has put up a pile of stones, but I'm uncertain nevertheless. Crying for protection just makes things worse, triggering their rage. Pay more attention to your phantoms, whose cold breath bears the stamp of anguish, creating your tailor-made retribution. Very few rules apply. Not much is left for rumination, but hands appear as though magically possessed, and you're sure again. This matters. I go back over my equipment. Salt smell pierces the irrelevant afternoon, and acerbic shadows cut up my thoughts into irregular dark chunks.

80
Diesel exhaust and harsh metals populate the deserts, but coefficients don't pencil out. I smell lacquer. At the appointed hour, I go forth, regardless. Repeated confrontations stir up the desired response. All systems go. If that's all it takes, then be my guest, at least until the millennium. Meanwhile, hearts and minds keep their distance. I turn my wrench so as to get it started, and all hell busts loose. Do a gut check and while there hash it out with the higher ups. No response, just dead air. Excuses, excuses. Try sorting that one out. Rage mounts like a rushing firewall. Then come the falsehoods, coated with historical slime. A retreat is sounded, as graves yawn open unburdening themselves.

81
Gird up thy loins, sons of the archon! An opening in the clouds sets free quivers of sunbeams, the golden shafts of eternity. Down in the hold a dynamo grinds and hums. As usual I'm trying to get somewhere else. My chances are slipping away. A meat cleaver crusted with dried blood turns up beyond the statute of limitations. If you confess early and profusely, your punishment will be adjusted along a sliding scale. Too late, some say. Even to consider such a request would take you to the cleaners, whereas my purpose here entails coming to terms with fleecing, not

approvingly. No, another rape victim racks up data points, and sobbing gets rudely discounted. My pathetic noises elicit fresh rounds of mockery. The entire carnival blows away in a stiff morning wind. I look back over a scintillating surface because certain genes are releasing their fumes. To call it a sphere amounts to purposeful distortion, but let's not mince words.

82
At the appointed hour a liveried butler holds a door, absolute and pointless, so that shoe leather and crystal can meet their destiny. Nothing doing. Your benefits have been terminated. Please hold. How so? Tired of the battle, I crawl off in mud and fashion myself a dream city. Computers boot up, then freeze. Listen up. I'm chopping at the core with full force, and humans go blithely about their business as if inferior worlds didn't even exist.

83
Who can assemble the remotest star, much less the mathematic of someone's soul? I summon up my waning courage and inch into the fray. Stray dogs sniff among garbage because they know, despite their misguided competition. Maybe you imagined a different outcome, one more congenial. Here you are. Wild wishes for surcease ensue, and jackhammers resume their impersonal arrangements. I register a crow, stricken because of its irrevocable message, as if to speak were to create. The pieces fall into place, substantiating the adage. I'm gambling with my life lived out among poor alternatives. Lungs and feet secure the deal, but insect intelligence mounts an effective counterstrike. Therefore, I conclude accordingly. Only a new object will have a shot, and that alone justified any effort, if justification be required. My metabolite balance skews, going into a yaw. Assessment is ongoing and irrelevant, so you'll have to deal. Winter clenches its iron jaw. Just getting out of bed precipitates an acute episode.

84
May their steroid levels burn through previous records, similar to clouds. My own searing shame becomes unbearable as I seek to

erase myself. People look away from me, from my structural stains. More comes up, an upheaval of slop and horror. I gather it in my withered arms in order to hide and pull back into the blessed dark. It's too soon. The deadening works itself into synaptic junctures. Home stabs my eyes. The rotting piles of Europe find their fate in their very decrepitude, mirror of sad consolation. This feels preferable to panic.

85
How little it takes for the seed to make it through, yet false promises abound, and then a storm gathers for a kind of demonstration. I see wolves. My thoughts pour out like water on packed ground, disappearing among stones. Mana from heaven. Slake my thirst before dusk, or gyrating ghosts will appear to haunt me. Mental gates slam shut forever. I suspect the worst, oxygenated plasma going bad. The war against filth and gore rages on unabated. Only the strategically flexible survive, and even this carries no guarantee. The internal meatus booms away, happily fulfilled, yet unscrambling alone is only the first step. Nothing develops. I'm drowning in a lake of pain. Lock pins were set way back when and voila! Each age bears a stamp, an incision that can be electronically transformed if you follow the pomegranate sees or gains of rice. First blood rites take precedence, until I go blank along with the rest, that is, the whole shooting match. Where can you find a cleft? Gigantic divisions plunge into the gap as flesh wilts and the populating is rendered mute.

86
Gratitude, like water, seeks its own level. After another meal alone, I go to bed, wondering about my paltry creation. Nothing personal. It's wouldn't be any different in your absence, just a structural disappointment. Now that beasts roam freely, I can adjust my scope accordingly, gazing out over smoldering ruins. Logical operations are sick and tired of pretending, so you end up back where you began. A sheet of ice extends its sovereignty, and nothing changes. Fractals take apart joists and I-beams until you shatter your last mirror. No, I can't say I would have picked this

set of bedeviled circumstances, but no choice was offered. Adapt or die. My preparations are complete. Whores and torture instruments go on display, but your calm bemused mien still strikes fear into their hearts. Envy corrodes the wiring, trips point from the walls.

87

All the subtlety goes unheeded in their mad rush to escape, but I've given up my claim to movement. Birds smash into plate glass. Lesser lights seize the reins, and the inclement weather exacts revenge. Someone operates a power drill, while virtue goes wholly unrewarded. Scraping and pounding finish the job. My gift is ignored, a figuring of the soul as days turn into years in a fluttering. Again, too late. Shutters crash down. Whatever heaps have been amassed will have to serve because sleep beckons. Custodial care costs. I'm aching in my bones. No human has touched me in seven years. Pack out the tools now that the job is done. Thankfully, my memory fails as the work force exits whistling up a storm. You never know. The core of neglect spreads like gas as tears leak out, burning my old cheeks. Words shrivel, turn to ash in my throat. Draw any conclusion you wish although a concussion will color your notions of correctness. No answer, so please press one. It's galling. Who is in charge? A beguiling melody issues from the interstices and tattoo parlors go bankrupt along with dry cleaners and bakeries. I lash out in vain. Superior forces carry the day, having staged a palace coup. After guy wires have been clipped, the all-out attack on fantasy begins in earnest. Repeated insults of nicotine abrade the epithelial lining. Storage facilities overflow with excess because night encroaches. More questions occur, and old loyalties are swapped for new, as yet untested ones.

88

Always the power structure inserts its tentacles, and once that magnetic pull snaps to, there'll be no more historical revision. Checking lists provides an alternative, and forced interaction stumps their best players. I return to my arsenal, desperate for better odds. Internal monitoring ticks on through the night. I've done little, in a sense. No one knows or can know. Shame keeps the pot at a simmer so as to implement proven tactics. The people have been subtracted through scalding, a cytokine storm. Waves roll through ether, and my homing device jams up again because of excess ozone. Frilly items float away, as I'm shunted aside if not actively spurned. Having no value, how can I go on?

89
My mind extends a claw, sinks it in, and drags. In this way the world goes lexical, until you drift into view. I realize how stunted, but what's that rustling? On and on, dust settles, obedient to its own loving rhythms. Faint echoes intersect with a more persistent grinding, none of which I can subordinate within my pyramids, so instead I have to accept what I'll never comprehend, the chattering of inhospitable creatures. Notice their stripes, smells of dried sweat and hallucinatory attacks being planned by candlelight. What were you expecting, a round of entertaining distractions for your daily routine, or perhaps some passing clarification? If so, what disappointment! While waiting, they elaborate more details because of sweetheart deals. I should know. Implications of guilt pollute an otherwise pure medium, so that getting a clear signal becomes laughable. No, who would have helped? Ascribing blame works, Legions of the damned come out of the woodwork like vermin.

90
They get their cut but don't take damages into account. Loss hurts, at least for a period until numbing sets in. The LED read-out points towards a resolution, or is that wishful thinking? DO others exist? Peripheral arterial defense falls over an edge where sea and sky meet. Yet I found myself resorting to the tried and true. No one wants to hear it, which I believe I understand, although you might convince me to the contrary. Brains in jars line shelves underground, and my carefully designed itinerary has to be asset aside. Natch. Any straight up version goes against the long-established protocol. Don't alter your course or reduce speed. Let's move some product.

91
An inner landscape unfolds, dark, depopulated, uneven. A tone or bush marks passage, as the way descends among undergrowth, a thin creek, insects. The ants are at war because it's their nature. I smell a bully. Chemicals reek, and squabbling over land or water rights comes with the territory. Wild dogs comb the city dump. Entitled Iranians ignore signs, which they imagine have to do only with others, so I say something. What can the virtuous complain about once their paunches are filled? Idiots enact legislation, and their pompous phraseology gets filed away under cover of darkness. Nothing short of obliteration will stem the tide. Babies are weeping up and down a hallway, their caretakers out on the landing for a smoke. Nothing out of the ordinary. There is more poetry in my little finger.

92
This is the room I'll die in. Strangers are sleeping in my house, so that a shotgun or Bowie knife might make a difference, although such a slow build-up all but guarantees heartbreak. Ventricular re-entry tachycardia spells trouble. Listen with every pore an ear. They'll haul it all off to the landfill, a history of pain covered with dust. Barely perceptible voices penetrate drywall and insulation. No one commanded it be thus and so. Who is the audience, a gathering of blathering fools? Frequently I return to earlier scenes that melt away on being envisioned, Salzburg, 1977. Where does a form take shape, emerging from the mass to grip my soul? Mist drifts across a still river, and the smells of autumn smoke ache deep inside. Autonomous entities preserve their status.

93
Off to the races. Extra helpings put you in a position of dependency, extracting commodities by guile. When chaos strikes, watch out for egalitarian tendencies, so to speak. You'll be incinerated in a trice. I'm clinging on. Guard dogs raise their snouts. Some deep restless yearning drives on, horrified at the possibility of crack-pate ramblings about the Bible. Try getting a fix, when parts blend and blur. If I show the wound, it will cut

deep, but in a split second feedback loops activate. A semblance endures. You can take stock afterwards, because gross weight readings require your undivided attention. Promises go underwater at that same rate, and I total them up for the nth time. At least a million have been marked, no small feat considering their resource limitations. Square roots and bottom lines compete for space at an intersection of air and meat. I stand by, no longer certain, and notice a grinding of gears because the hour has struck unbeknownst. Visions of wheels lit up like forest fires crack that ancient code, secrets of ruined lives salted away until they turn to ash. The bellowing of doom, again and again.

94

Where shall I look for traces of my own minor key? Count them, if that matters. Ignorance leads to a sure catastrophe, end of the line. Since I told you, I have no more liability. Get it down in writing. Just because you've alluded to an extreme unction makes for a poor excuse, but soldier on. Killing is thrilling. Reverse force fields so that passive children can sleep even though jackals are combing the outskirts, getting closer by the minute. Lies about money abound, and tyranny spreads like lymphoma because of a wiring failure. Resentment replaces milder forms of benign tolerance, so get ready because I'm next. Let them duke it out. I'm running down alleys barefooted and furious. Exchanges won't do it. An elaborate figure is carved into the surface over a long period, and death rattles haunt the very atmosphere. A cabinet contains letters, an awl, various punches for metalwork, and cheap crockery.

95

Pneumatic drills and hammers kick into action because another monster in the making strafes the beach with heavy artillery fire. Only one master switch controls those circuits so I kiss off hundreds of dollars before dawn. Waves go under, despite your ingenious forms of protest. Play it safe and still end up dead, even as you long pointlessly after the light that is going away. Brown skin deflects their barbed sticks with ease, and mythological creatures lumber into view, huffing and stamping. Simple understand evades police sweeps conducted before sunrise. Figures in marmoreal relief threaten to squeeze the life out of their immediate surroundings, yet don't, and a wind blows in off the permanent desert. Paths never cross. Smeared blood gives them away, and I cry in futility. A justifiable distrust of authorities is beside the point. Craft and guile grease those skids. Bile issues from various portals, poisonous gases, the damaged language of an end game.

96
Some would have it that madness and reason are linked, but not in the sweet inner structure of a living being. Machines are stripped of their innards, and that kind of concentration goes to the boards. Eyes empty themselves out. Precise measurements echo that in-dwelling rage, but only until no more repair can count because of lipid build-up and a core grief. Shipwreck. Standardized sweat breaks through, without any external propping up. Database searches hum throughout, and cost analysis brands their hides. Steady application swells ranks until the bursting point. As if. Filaments or threads manage to insinuate themselves into the corpus callosum, eventually breeching the amygdala and hippocampus. Tried and true tools bring home the bacon. I wait on the sidelines, bereft, lonely.

97
Tobacco, urine, engine grease. At the moment of delivery, childhood fantasies extract their due in that cold calculus. Small-town hicks and yokels curl up nevertheless, and prairie breezes ache with uncontrolled nostalgia because the heart cares not for irrelevant details. A subjection freezes their little joys, preparing them for export. After all, what about wine and high heels, the mash that generates? Upstream or downstream, you don't see that much of them any more because of the beck and call. A daily practice advances, but policing the premises will scare up dinner. Word filters back, trickles down. You learn the hard way and against certain odds cast your line, but impetigo gums up the works. Inertia sets in stolidly. I feel helpless again, doomed and crushed.

98
Each slab falls into place. Unethical behavior summons a djinn. Snakes slither out of water, climb nearby trees. When all else has failed, they come. Laying on of hands, some with knives, tells a different tale. They hang loosely from branches and evoke a numen. Where have the ancestors gone? A sickening lassitude overcomes me, and fellow travelers fall by the wayside. Count the tree rings, or imagine their surprise when you tell them, because a flow of smoke or infected flies darkens the morning skies. Passivity becomes protest. A blanketing green covers canyons, and I'm awestruck, anxious. The paraphernalia fade so that I can enter.

99
Gulls screech out their baleful mourning. Time for the return trip. Now what? A huge feeling roils, and pounding plays havoc with your diminishing eyesight. A musical phrase identifies that perpetrator, whose ultimate clock face reads blank. But you try. Circuit boards snap into their proper slots, ready for fresh plasma. I assess conditions subjectively and resolve to cast my lot, but internal controls need tweaking. You become a figurehead instead of pockmarked and set aside. My mind grinds through because of an alignment or conjunction. Meanwhile, a semi-fictional account works its brand of magic, and hayseeds and bumpkins loll about in the barn. Am I next? You have to wonder. Gawking at utensils and finery will suck out your élan vital.

100
I have no commercial value. Halitosis and dandruff plague that group until they capitulate. An uncomfortable conjecture rattles their cages, just one more among a slew. The planet contemplates its options and chooses too take the easy way out. I hanker and wheedle in vain. Greed and envy carry the day. Reverberating disks transmit a sequence of signals, despite mine disasters and government coups. At last capitalists get their come-uppance. Open criticism falls easily under that rubric because the transmission towers keep the ball rolling. Damp flesh just wants to get by. Fat rolls impede fluidity, unremarkably, so that to

complete the task takes twice the effort. Get on with it. Digital reality, you say, but I'm not so sure because the fecal stick or vomit bolus may cast the deciding vote. I walk pointedly towards that shadow.

101
Blessed silence descends, spreading its sweet extirpation. Whoever cannot penetrate must be absorbed. Children stain the air with their footsteps, and you bark and howl. My magical operations have lost their bite, so I lie down amidst trash and leavings.

102
Serendipity isn't the word. A monstrous hunger crosses that scarred landscape, baying madly. I jot down coordinates, then steal a furtive glance. The smell of snow sets loose a wall of grieving. What couldn't be said but released its heavy metals into the water table? That raw transaction proves prescient, bringing all their fondest wishes to fruition. A sense or notion supplants common thinking, and there is no more wondering, just distant thunder or bombing. Catecholamines rush to their gateways, lock on. I wake up in fear. Soon I will be alone again, staring into the blackness. Ancient queens realign at their leisure, borne along on others' backs. Once a year the sky implodes, and crude coats wildlife. The gyroscope slows, wobbles tiltingly. Personal integrity conceals a broth, although your cache of days holds out hope. Softened footfall conveys a mysterious air, drawing attention to radar printouts and electronic junk heaps. Pinball ratchets up your investiture, stirring though that proclamation may be. My rhythm fits an agricultural calendar, shooting out over mine fields and swimming holes. Fog emanates from eye sockets. I strain against leather straps as the beatings proceed with a mechanical and impersonal coldness. Sometimes I notice enough coherence to be able to get a fleeting orientation, but cysts form and spread rapidly. Fire trucks skid to a stop, their coiled hoses crashing down in roiling piles. If I'm not there I can't be attacked yet.

103
Virtue and manual dexterity lay a foundation. Accoutrements fall to the wayside, made irrelevant by an atomic explosion. I'm spinning my wheels within wheels so as to tread water and go for the gold. As I notice a crossing of the blood-brain barrier, tiny ripples become bigger until voices drown me out. What does that feeling connote? No more game-playing. Bone meal rolls off conveyor belts, and I sweat it out, stunned by their arrogance and indifference. The Acropolis echoes down the ages, battered by wars and the elements. If there is any exploration going on, it's right here, or nearby, because fantasy maps have served their purpose, stupidly, and must now be destroyed. But who volunteers to play executioner now that history has been transformed? Just what I thought: the harshly anaclitic depression has eviscerated the animal.

104
Perhaps a prone position might extend the franchise, vibrating bolts free. My imagination runs wild. Those who can no longer work get cooked. I'm dead serious. Affect regulation, self-soothing, brittle object relations, you name it. Petty thievery gradually replaces grand larceny and subtle punishment. Blood drains out. Recombinant technology predicts a wasting away, from which you cannot hide in food. Fake jolly belly laughs merely postpone the whizzing blade, as you will soon learn. Get it over with. Tree removal sticks in my craw. Landings are staged so as to stave off catastrophe. I think I knew my own preferences, swept up in the thickness. No one has gotten one iota further, so I wait it out, making the occasional sarcastic aside to let off steam. Thrust and parry as I might, the markets roar on. A grim visage doesn't bode well. Ugly rain slams rooftops and asphalt, and calculating rates won't alter them a smidgeon. Bingo.

105
Without adequate grown factor, their articulated concerns wash away, leaving tracks or scars, depending. Hirsutism pursues its quarry in an always provisional universe, worked out monthly because of social practice. I slip in and out, not quite in control,

but keeping focused on sodium excretion numbers. Making minor fixes, I'm deluded. Lions know that score. Endless speculation in an upward spiral stumps your studio audience, who moan loudly on cue. Ball bearings chip in, and cheap shots miss the mark, because claims of ignorance can't woo them. The prison managers fall to the far left on an autism spectrum. I see this, realizing the usual impotence that accompanies displays of extreme power. Baseball bats get involved, even at a sit—down black-tie event. I retreat into my mind's most distant corners. Water carriers hump on through, although acid-base rations vary accordingly. I'm monitoring the situation.

106
Now the codes apply. Tilt-a-whirl statistics spin out of control, sending up smoke signals, but who am I to judge? Incomplete forms pack heat, as I grease their chambers, then notice I'm doing my best to chase or follow a small moving object across a field. Sickening envy fells them, whereas I go on as before. Too late. You have to fit their demographic profile. Patience and brinksmanship pay off, although belonging to a cabal certainly can't hurt. Meanwhile, nobler sentiments garner only a passing nod. You have to lust after it, even slavishly. Otherwise, why do they stay in the hunt? Unalloyed love, you say? I think not. Layers of insulating material interfere. But whose mine shaft will pop that question? These arrangements were made eons ago, back in the Permian. Time-lapse rushes things along, and I slide a shoulder under the weight. A weary sun creeps up, despite having vanquished its eternal enemy again. We both know it's not over and that traipsing around will come back to haunt you. The delicate structure of morning creaks as those who are able oil their weapons while dreaming of happier times.

107
The ones who survive fit the bill. I'm reeling in lines, only to lower them into a cavern. Somewhere beneath the biosphere, boiling and slashing lay down the law, and fortune's wheels grind the world to sludge. I'm sifting through it because God said so and in English no less. I step out onto the afternoon plaza just like so

many others, giving myself over fully to the illusion, which becomes real. Do you see those apples, that wrought iron? How else can love be declared?

108

Testing continues, and failing when daylight asserts its dominion. I can't pretend otherwise but set aside those tools and recede into utter unremarkable banality. It's living invisibly. Veils of fantasy fall away, leaving a core of pain. No wonder I can't touch you as it would kill me. The pitiful deities who arrange these diversions are cancer. Cascading enzymes take me through the straits towards that archipelago. Moisture condenses, trickling down cark in crooked rivulets while cold fog hangs among upper branches. Seasons flit by as I'm hurled into another dimension. Hold the phone there. Whose dream claims ownership? My mind hovers, advancing along floorboards early in its sad career, but connecting cables are clogged and tangled. Someone pulled the plug in advance. In between explosions, silence. I dip my head in a river, then study a shifting panorama, hoping against hope.

109

Many hands have participated, thereby eliminating any individual stamp, but why quibble when cumulus and blossoming cannot? Premature exclamations pour out, and I change gears because white skin wants its way. There is always a way you can twist it to make it look the way you want, and I squeeze through that narrow aperture again. If I don't admire the star, I must turn away. A checkerboard of options spreads itself out as time-controlled electronic locks snap shut in unison. The craggy brow and steely stare complicate matters, as though encouraged nevertheless. I look out over the city before speeding downhill to plunge fully clothed in water. No one cares. Roadways and passages between buildings casually absorb foot traffic, and war plots are hatched as if one had nothing to do with the other. Experience counts. Poor-mouthing won't cut it, so check your gear carefully before boarding. Twangs and drawls nurture a bond. Slight pressure does the trick, but goofballs and lollygagging add spice. I review their summaries with an eye to nuclear triggers since family life achieves its poignant trajectory unassisted and uninfluenced. Cations and anions are perfectly capable of finding their way. Who needs whom in this little minuet? Even that concept cannot go unscathed, so I assemble fishing tackle, humiliated by their constant rejections.

110
I use the minimum and render myself unnoticeable. Maybe I'll skate through, although to what end? Published train schedules seem dry but are aching. Country stations ooze a poisonous nostalgia. I'm running and running, looking for a particular street number, 68986, and will be late. It's a fresh, green university campus near low bluffs. None of this matters, but who knows? I'm the one spinning out my own fate, only to be grasped later when it may be too late. The pieces recombine, as I draw a bead but can't hold my focus long enough. Language loosens a notch until you question its very ontology. The State Department gives itself a certain air. Over time a formula emerges, boring newcomers who want action. Once you get your way, why should you give a shit?

111
Yes, the grain is coarse. Volcanic smoke blankets the globe, grounding air travel. Welcome to limbo. My skin is repulsive, marred with red lesions. As soon as it's dawn, I move on, and each stroke is ab ovo. Just because of an absolute and irrevocable limit, I'm not forced to live on the husks of memory. Instead, my old hands feel their way along. A massive anvil of gray sky flattens out the early morning light, and human frailty gasps for breath at the slightest effort. I pause by the trickling waters, fishing, as it were. Nothing is biting. The taut drumhead goes dead, distended with excessive heat. Ancestral traces droop and fade. Another chilly mausoleum exhales its rank odor as though challenging my right. Softly, softly a door closes, and nutrients run their course towards metabolites and necrosis. It's a sure thing. Gnarled roots dive deep into a spirit world huge with its own expectancy. Giant spiders dangle from branches among which I must climb on my

way through. Alveoli go about their business, and further identifications, parchment, and documents troll these waters.

112
Strip searches follow routine questioning because of nationalistic hatreds. These hours achieve their richness simply through reflection, a fact that becomes quickly obvious. Take your pick. When their cheeks go out, forget about it. A need for punishment trumps all comers. You seem to feel you've come home at last. I'll go on missing you until the pain subsides, and I can hear Bach again. Some nifty calculations set the score straight, so that obsessive planning can impede catastrophe. Little did I know. Arraignment is eternal, and sucking it up benefits only bankers with pot bellies and antler sets mounted on cabin walls. You know the drill. My flimsy excuse can't hold up but looks to bust a gut laughing. Somehow I make it through, uncertain about particulars, whereas changes are noted and entered for safe-keeping or subsequent study. Peripheral edema? Undaunted, I strain overly. A flame-thrower rests by the door, just in case, and past horrors recede. Hogs root through their slop. The utter sameness both reassures me and absorbs my screams. Ownership bypasses their elaborate controls, bringing home the bacon so that as usual tidal variations can't cause excessive damage.

113
Monsters haunt me at night, exacting a toll for my existence, until you gather up your belongings and head for any remaining hills. I'm scanning police frequencies now. I never got beyond that neglect. This has become my world, a small yard, relative silence. Soon they'll set me free, and you will figure out how to go on. Always their niggling questions about the cost of objects eat away at my biological arrears. Look at the rhythms if you really want to know. Forceful agencies stalk the abused land. I'm wrenched apart at sunrise, plunged into cold horror of what I've done, of what's been done to me. Who has to walk there despite stinging reproaches, a death knell of prices and bar codes? This is who I am.

114
All well and good, but let's not forget. Proceed calmly to the observation deck. Unless fireflies and mosquitoes die out, simple facts will cry out for revenge. But grander moves are afoot, and you ponder a quality that will always elude your expression. Finally, you accept what's most pitiable and buckle down to making money or dismissing it. The neighbor's cur barks, and off in the distance freeway traffic pursues its aimless tail. After you've explained yourself a million times, it comes automatically. Soft voices imply human concerns. Then all goes silent. Breaking into the big time, you push for the fame you crave. Television chatters and blathers as the alcohol works its way through channels. Moreover, they trot out their nostrums on cue. Everything is on hold. Comfort, an old frame hunched over its instrument, hawks wheeling for pleasure, who can regulate a universe, regardless of its longing? My bones resorb, going out of phase. Feet stamp dirt, but now it's for other ends entirely.

115
Up and down inside a locked machine, I'm pointed towards an unattainable galaxy. Desultory rain doesn't so much fall as languish, surly and stupid, in sluggish air. I set off in my boat, unsure as usual about what awaits me despite lengthy preparation. The ugly stolidity of these walls dares me, and you , to dream of other climes, but whose concoction will you quaff when the hour strikes? Everything holds steady. I'm lashed to the mast, so to speak, coated with H. pylori drilling for gold. Promises of exceptional value trail in the incessant polls, but so what when each tentative step spins off billions of ions. Muscles launch worlds of shifting axes, the sky bowl rolling overhead. Rank necrosis announces itself with a somber quality. Not to comply produces its own brand, and a wall of debris is rapidly erected against a flood of bone chips, trabecular chunks. I'm geared down, nose in the dirt. Wishing won't make it so, but a serpent certainly gets attention, revving the engine hours into it. A syndrome of sunlight and dull, incessant pain would call for suspicion in the differential diagnosis. How else can nodules and polyps populate their domain, if not by some complicated

feedback routes detectable only on afterthought? Recursive lines play it safe. Don't expect to maintain integrity unless you risk it, because intracranial pressure pushes the dipstick. Hustle along, or perish.

116
Very few pathways remain, so I have a tighter selection. This is what it has taken, anemia or gastritis. Imagining any other fissure sucks the life out because celebrations are state-controlled. At the crack of dawn tin soldiers line passageways, blocking access. Is that what you want to hear, after drinks on a warm verandah? Justice wails and keens. An occipital fracture completes the picture, and automatic horses' asses can't help themselves. Four solid hours later Hypnos rules the roost. Fanciful constructions push out mortar, nails, and glue, darkening my small knowledge even further until I'm lost altogether. Strontium 90, you say? Get more face time or their whereabouts will vanish, leaving no encrustation or signs of activity. I'm winking, of course, but when will milk trucks and TD-24s be retired?

117
Strong disapproval matters little. Cooler heads grab the limelight, so that organized opposition doesn't stand a chance. Multiple miniature fistulas pock tubing, jamming a rod in the sprockets. Angry wives tear open confidential correspondence. You bet. Your cold fingers talk. Manifold exhaust fumes top those charts whereas the mind can't stop cranking out its tripe. Safety first, it goes, so you breath easy, but I still have to face jibs and blows. Stones pelt my back. Naturally, I decide to leave town, taking my colored pencils. Thoreau can stay behind, along with Mary Baker Eddy. Your misfiring hypothalamus calls those shots. Let me be clear. Even a demanding and indifferent world is preferable o the evil I now. You go about your business, feathers unruffled, and my compass spins erratically before going into a coma.

118
Liquids recede, then advance, repeating a cycle. Honey and tar sound an alarm. I wait it out, again, listening to pitch-blend,

putty, hinges that bind evening to night. Always their muffled cries, always a drumbeat of slow agony they lovingly installed.

119
Like a diseased dog I'm listlessly sniffing through forgotten garbage and cachexis. Fruit flies dive-bomb, hook through steam and rot. Look lively. Think? Metaphysical shambles cripple the enterprise, but some blind urge keeps pushing despite my futility. Soon it's real money. Fake laughter hangs in stale indoor air, and connective tissue is soaked in old synovial fluid. Periodic checks can't hurt. Try back later. Smear campaigns get results, so that fat layers just pinch the right nerve. Fuck the government, shamelessly. Cow dung litters pastures because no one cares. How else can I be used? My feet slur through grass and memories. Petty theft and fear of open wounds take to the hills or go underground, depending. I follow textures, their unique warp and woof, hungry for cloud cover or a stand of palms gently swaying, telling myself I can be happy at some point. Public information adds a dollop or pinch, but look at the real rates of change. Moisture slickens walkways, as though your craving could ever be satisfied. At least you get to consort with your kind, whereas I can't pretend.

120
All these things exist outside of history, despite its official blandishments. Thighs of brass, blaring horns, tambourines stir the dead air, and a spirit knocks me down. I beg for help, but can't get past a row of cash registers. Outside? It's possible to entertain the notion. Skip your hypotheticals. It hurts to hear the seagulls, but chilly stares remind me who I am. Concupiscence of the eyes I nullify by looking at dirt, drainage ditches, cracked culverts, heat-baked woodpiles. If anyone is around you'd never guess, given these deserted streets and smell of rotting weeds. Gas exchange ratios determine your fate, and the pH balance. My name closes the ion channels. A paralyzing indifference seeps in like noxious vapors, failed music now heard only on the promenade on Sunday afternoon to reinvigorate animals.

121
What morose lucubrations, dragging down misery, lumber along disorganized and sloppy with pity, infiltrate their environs? Regulators are watering at their chops. I kick open a barroom door and breast the crowd, then crawl back to safety. A knot forms in my throat. Calculi accrete in darkness, far from the deafening roar. Nature exacts its due before casting you aside with casual grace if not abandon, as triumph returns the favor. No, I'll pass on that one and be content to go on rubber-necking to the grueling end. Dumbfounded. Who wouldn't be? Eating clocks sinks a putt, and my vainglorious posturing pays twisted homage, taking umbrage. Repositories of dead rage await judgment day as my trembling limbs flail about, looking for any old purchase. Harness hobbles me, and abstract freedoms being merchandised. They move product, keeping themselves busy. One dilemma supersedes another.

122
Clinical wisdom would have it otherwise, despite slaughterhouses and anticoagulants. My abrasion repels, in the spirit of archaic rituals. Cool breezes pick out a narrative thread, a loose screw. Rash conclusions, but that's life, always about to jump the gun. I waste another trip, then blame fate or the banking system. Because of depleting stores, your exit strategy has to be redesigned. The puffed cheeks of winter seem oddly reassuring so I savor the moment, oblivious and grateful. Ipanema glosses over violent assaults, graft, and mendacious flattery. Crippling pain doubles me over, then peripheral neuropathy. Popping the question at thirty grand a pop is out of the question. It is what it is, never having been in any vanguard. Emblematic, no? I undergo flaying just by stepping outside and noticing a quality of afternoon, pentagrams drawn on asphalt in chalk. Nothing adds up, but I suppose that's their point, whoever they are. Precious objects speak in riddles but only to those who can hear. A ghost pours hot lead into my ears. Chapter and verse form a spindle, so that the truth can out.

123
Horse carcasses litter the adjacent fields, so I insert myself among still warm intestines. Weird images hammered into bone take on a coloring I don't understand. Tattered voices train. Cockeyed drunks howl at the flat-assed moon, which will never suffer from the Coxsackie virus or carpal tunnel. I see elements of a face, enough to give me the willies. At the witching hour they rebuild another engine and counter-sign contracts, but who inflicts the most telling blows?

124
Sex behind closed doors pats them down for concealed weapons. What about you and your counterfeit identity? Threshing machines lack panache. Critical breasts are subpoenaed to appear before a grand jury, but secret conversations recorded on calendar pages fade into a blank physics of pure amnesia. Royal dastardly deeds sketch out their possibility as players although consummate wrestling slams the mat. A signet ring stalls out, infected by the symbols that could be salvaged as I give myself over to a dialectic of shout and whimper. Bare feet tread in pleasure, eager to survive. Whether or not I'm aware, teratologists work between well demarcated zones, wanting only to be done with grieving. Spring holds itself up as an example. My squeaks attract the wrong kind of attention. Colostomy bags reserve the right to refuse service based on color or creed. Even though I have been apprised, my sphere of influence shrinks.

125
Then back, as a cycle swings through, I'm launched again down rails, all highly controlled by absentee landlords. Feeling understood initiates a chain reaction, and the classic harrowing turns up curious evidence, such as digits planted in soil presumably for a purpose. Square one. My face has petrified. Underground swimming is a lost art. Do not pass go. Batches of data roll into view, but I can't perform the alignment. I'm too old, or this is how it's always been. Get used to their impositions. Squamous cell hyperplasia fouls its nest, and micrometric procedures hold the fort. I smash apart my grandiose passivity

with sonar and a ball-peen, but check out their deadline, flagged for demolition by federal flunkies. What implicit rules govern these metastases? Cranial hemorrhage positions plastic explosives so that pustules and plaque can stem the tide or die trying. Why save their invoices when a sausage-maker's only passion pounds ingredients to a paste? Belief abuts reality. I can't quite catch my breath, as dysphagia blocks the tunnel, diverting nautical traffic. Curmudgeons need not apply.

126
Cultural sickness crapes, then scolds whatever it touches. Military procurement exacerbates fragility until cracks appear along struts. Too much work. Factory output maxes out, and cold food bequeaths its nutrients. Unspeakable acts precede my doubting and prevarication, but within the system greatness will prevail. Pipes go around, as I nod off. Vasculitis and impetigo chime in, give their two cents. Sharing food capitulates, as though fisheries and aviaries had answers. This far in, there is no turning back. Black widows glare and bide their ever-loving time. In order to erect a semi-permeable membrane, I thread a series of needles. Wild boar burst in. Soon enough disturbances recur. What can I do? Whining and blabbering penetrate my walls, wishing for that mythical pot of gold. A pattern crumbles away, falling to the beach below, and a circle of tiny creatures widens, then contracts. I ask a series of unanswerable questions as social arrangements congeal. Software patches infect septal dividers, but I still must correlate slabs of regenerating flesh before drafting my report. If you think it's easy, try it. Flatulence and botulism lie in wait. A Mercator projection will outlast your best endurance record, and using age as your excuse won't hack it. I'm wrapping this one up, labeled and numbered for ready reference because the customer is king, and cash speaks loud and clear. Sociopathy glitters. An accurate estimate jams the wheels of industry, spreading welts for special emphasis.

127
Eclampsia threatens to end the line, and helicopters deliver their eagerly awaited cargo. Green apples foretell a fruitful harvest,

despite hypertension and edema. Dew glistens on grass blades. The exact setting evades ready formulation, and fortunately so because those who lay claim hope to wear down any opposition. My mind empties, and the whole phantasmagoria evaporates. Oh, that's different. Blood thickens at junctures and narrowings, until calcium channels snap to. At ease. As you were. Common carriers include rather unlikely candidates. An unearthly glow emanates, and reverse thrusters fog up windows. For some reason I am caught on the horns, but you can't expect any less, or the classic triad of symptoms alerts control panels. I bear down on my tools because other options have been foreclosed. Watchful waiting imbues their prognostication with a vision, a mirror reflection. Acrobats talk their way out of speeding tickets, as stew sloshes around. Again, word comes down that you'll have to score your pain with more attention to detail. Americans expect a free pass. Very few assassins join snipers with their morbid intimacies, loving eyes, and trigger fingers. Off-shore winds keep me in the loop until I notice how much I've aged by making hypothetical comparisons. Pneumonia comes a-calling, all innocent-like. Where can I find that set of gradated lenses almost a month afterwards?

128

Gore drips to the ground. Valves shut, then open, keeping flows moving along. All that generation of females failed, and most of the males. A simple protein surplus aches for hours, going well beyond the bounds of duty. Shame plays its trump, and it matters not if you don't care. You'll take your cherished dermatitis with you for the ride. Violets, petunias, and carnations mask a tale of entropy, so tropical sprue or jejunitis fells an empire unbeknownst to the proud owner. Be the first on your block, no questions asked. I observe these processes and incorporate them into my repertory of stock figures. Finding proper mathematical axioms certainly does no harm, but who can assemble enzymes? Maybe your adjustable rate mortgage will get canned, or maybe not. Defenses shoot up all over the place. I'm tired. Prothrombin time establishes a multiplier so that glass vials can be held firmly in place.

129
Please, spare me protracted good-bye speeches. I left, against my puny will, way back when, and their intolerance burns itself into a living substrate. It's an alloy. Just let your cells regenerate, and cinch them down with latigos, because there is no peace to be disturbed. Let's get one thing clear. Nostalgia or a wish, constructed agencies throw their hats in the ring. You'll be beaten to a pulp by cold judges awaiting gangrene. This is the extent of damage, hard evidence that it happened. Eternal warfare blankets airwaves, and childhood games portend a dark future, until I reconstruct a forgotten past, thereby closing that circuit. Mammograms render verdicts while the chorus looks on stupefied. My natural curiosity takes another body blow.

130
Drug cartels muscle their way in, and only the lonely lament in style. I've become a connoisseur of dirt and little creatures, old air, bilirubin-stained urine. Coring and husking have their own rhythm, a signature in lymph. Angry clocks are screaming my name, releasing a holding pattern. Ablation might work, to buy some guns, but then what? Amassed gemstones launch a counterattack by ground and sea, and stragglers pin their waning hopes on sheer fantasy. Buccal ulcers seal that deal, so that you know for a dead certainty that collectors are well on their way, their very cells having memorized directions, wind speeds, seasonal shifts in humidity.

131
Well, what do you know. It's a slam-dunk case of little import, but tracking butterflies calls for patience and intuition. Let's go fishing for example, or bare-handed hunting, if you can imagine. I'm breaking stones and being broken or a least drummed out of town for who knows what bogus charges. Off the main drag you'll see another stratum. I abide with loving open arms to receive them, regardless, and most arrive exhausted or in great fear. The jig is up. Plenary session limps on despondently as I slink out. The body goes up in flames as if some grand sensorium in the sky had that expanded capacity, until I refocus and notice a mausoleum,

sad tree trunks, an utterly meaningless carpet design. Why go on? As they leave I wall myself in with fragile paper, crystal, handwriting of deceased ancestors. Dried sweat, cigar smoke, wax, heroin steal back in because prone passivity leaves you baffled and steaming. Twenty minutes later you plunge in. Their branding irons are glowing, poised to strike. In all actuality, you're done. Crows bear stigmata, and my advance tears are their own defense.

132
Elation spikes, then wanes, and a dense thicket is thrown up. These ligatures are the closest parallel. I'm on the lookout, but purity is a horizon upon which doomed crosshairs are trained. It hurts me, and I undo pieces so that no more juice can run down those tubes. Fields fold, creating spaces that echo the dark kingdom's cave complex. Who goes there? Faint wisps float by, and the little ones scamper for safety. Syrup cloys as my thoughts clabber, caught in a thromboxane cascade. Lights signal your imminent departure, a shiver of rainwater on your skin. It slaps the hull, lolling and lulling because who wants to go? Electrolyte balances tilt and sway. What would you do different?

133
Search out the bunghole because an apocalypse of phase shifting spikes your spokes. Numerology comes to seem logical as polysaccharides harden into shells. Hordes flood the pipelines as you muse on blithely, even wearily towards late afternoon once drinks are passed around. It's the custom in these parts to extract a tooth or chop off a digit at puberty. Haunted houses demand a tariff, as the alphabet chokes you unconscious. This is it. Indecipherable laughter ricochets from synthetic barriers as I pack ball bearings. Once more, with feeling. Following, I find myself constrained to repeat. Careful listening for supraventricular fibrillation develops a hypothesis. Figure-ground reversals confuse hypertension with disrespect, leading to less than ideal leakage.

134
If I can do it, will piecemeal techniques still be so humiliating? Hunger for shadows answers to no one. My capacities erode, as the blinds come down, until my muscles jerk involuntarily: catabasis head-first down into darkness. I await some form of release, not to be corrected by leaving money in a corner, or throwing a hissy fit. The matter has become more complex, and I've eased up on the brake pedal. Then it's all forgotten, as if it never existed. Snakes slither away. A barren smoking scene of destruction greets unwary passersby, although elsewhere caterwauling competes with law enforcement. Penny-ante boneheads and stumblebums come crawling out at night, sucking up God's own precious oxygen, oblivious to the condition of its very possibility. Instead, love butchers a carcass. How can you expect any other response, given their Byzantine tax code and rhetoric about human rights? Empires go into free-fall as the water table sinks, and I kiss my chances good-bye. Forward my file on, if you don't mind, because of a legally binding arrangement with its authorized codicils. Who is perfect?

135
Strippers horrify their parents for pay. Sometimes I gasp for air under the rain of blows, and a shred looks out beseechingly. What at first glance seems solid trembles pitifully even though there is no breeze. Such a slow rate of change cannot be perceived, yet armchair philosophers and generals enjoy pontificating. My legs have been cut off below the knees. If you listen, you can detected a murmur of backwash through a calcified mitral valve. Burnt offerings placate your rage-prone deity, who especially loves human sacrifice because of its power-augmenting capacity. Underneath, fear. Finally I get revenge although only in fantasy. Nerve conduction pathways play havoc with your sidekick. A narcoleptic lassitude descends, and the entire village population retreats for another afternoon.

136
Haul ass to your inner sanctum. Youth is fleet of foot, and an organic door bills itself as superior to casual contenders, but I'm

not so sure. Lent sublimates your autonomous meat. They have a veritable stranglehold on me. Indiscriminate rape and torture, malignant psychopathy, a witch's brew of disconnected rubble gets carted off for disposal, and yawning stops them in their tracks. Cocaine supply lines pull it off. They throw out a sop, but I'm not biting because knowledge is power, and don't talk back. I stay behind so that you can learn to speak your mind more forcefully. My neck graces the chopping block. Beyond the breakwater you can spot spinnakers, as clouds scud in a brisk wind. All that and more. Castles conjure up your latest business bubble. Willful ignorance has an affect identical to congenital. Chunks of skin flake off, until ambassadors are recalled. Photocopies are scattered about, yet whether afferent or efferent, sealant and fresh gauze pay out line. I'm carving a niche because I want to pass on my code, but hemodynamic instability builds its case. Can you insert a fuse? No single shot proves that an alert moon has it made. Fiddling with food blows a whistle.

137
But their Catherine wheels work their magic, and the Pope dresses like a woman, but numbed minds steeped in liquor pour blood in the fosse. Their fontanels never quite measure up, so I polish my handle and seize intellectual property right and left. Now you know. Flattery and simony grate on your nerves, despite battalions rushing into formation. Annexing sex is next. What the hell. Any portal will do when it comes to S. aureus. Just ask your doorman, who has all the answers. Hair and flesh on fire, I rush screaming from the bathroom. A stoic countenance comes only much later, after years of pleading that produce zilch.

138
I see the same hotel stairways and streets of a foreign city. There is some vague sense of a train or buss connection looming. Neutrophils and basophils come crashing in to set up a wall, and I roll over, unaware. Wear them down through endurance. My tiny evanescent mind pictures gives solace in a storm of nauseating data. Old wooden street cars with their 30-watt bulbs and can-backed seats rocket through working-class suburbs, all within the

city sprawl. An anthropological survey destroys ritual mounds, dragging secret practices into its maw, and my concrete references are drained of their vital fluids by a series of aluminum pumps and yellow rubber hoses. It seems wholly otherwise, but whose psychotic core spins down its black dynamo? Your ass in a deadlock, clamped and bolted to the ground, stops the clock. You can hear their teeth gnashing and the powerful sick moans of mortally wounded information files. I stare out an anonymous window that seals out moisture and dust. Penile jets nose around crowded tarmac fields, but where are the necessary cleavers, steel filings, axel grease, cotton bales? My longing shades into panic. The humdrum kit and caboodle throws you for a loop, and an overseer cracks the whip. Nevertheless, you levy charges as though only your own salvation were at stake.

139
Coal mines gobble up centuries. Amniotic baths precede real purification until their pretensions do them in. I was duped at the outset. Hurry to triage. Unexplained absences contribute a serving of murk. For a few moments I'm off that grid and on another. My blasting license has expired, so that illicit acts scare them off, but of course they return, heavily armed and loaded for bear. Sons become fathers. Pressurized cabins dart around, as I total various columns in my head, but please don't tell. Most figures want an undue share, which they can't appreciate anyway. As a result you break bones. You are arrested for vagrancy, for breathing. Excuses seem thin indeed although inorganic compounds bust a gut. This is all I ever wanted to do, tell you what's inside. Josiah Wedgwood wreaks havoc, as hearses proceed through deserted streets. I let waves wash over me, pretending an assent I don't really command, but it's my way of blending in. Cock rings and dildos freeze solid in blocks of ice, another chapter in a failed autobiography.

140
Such riches must go unrewarded, so I'm subtracted formally because of jet-fuel contract violations. I'm combing fine print

myopically. That's news to you? Titled nobility get their druthers. Be that as it may, chow hounds have to suck it up. Brainwashing comes with a hefty price tag, but you already recognize what it takes to slay an enemy who is sleeping or too young for self-defense. Vengeance is mine, saith the CEO. Check your glycemic index. Church music depresses them, extracting a confession of heinous sins. Some day I'll look back. But you've got to deal with water, and my face stays put. Smells of coffee and new snow duel with night vapors in distant cities I can assume once existed. Do names matter, except to attorneys at law? Here I am free, paradoxically if viewed from a certain angle. Degrees of pitch become critical, not a matter to be treated lightly.

141
I don't, cognizant of scars and serum. Pickled souls stare out of their jars in the museum basement. What are you so fearful of, if not their ears plugged with wax? Dried out leather shuffles along concrete corridors in the half-light, and "Danny Boy" faces the music. There are no tomorrows. Mortal offense bears its grudge with great honor, and carbines or muskets carve a fetish until dollars run out. Trains arrive and depart with stunning regularity. Tawdry curtains barely impede sickly light, while oblivious Asians dream their way deeper into a cultural disjunction. Shouting guts your shotgun. I'm back at the tiller, never left. Webbing expands secretly, silently, because denizens hibernate so they can transcend gravity.

142
Different levels of penetration set the scene, and surface dodges slowly give way. I'm taking depth soundings. A single dust mote flickers and fades. You extend your hand, so full of longing, into a void, and concubinage repeats its damaged fairy tale. Do you see? A coating blocks out light, and vitamin deficiency causes me to cringe. Crash dummies have a fighting chance at alleviating a drastic situation. Even a monolith would make your hatred more palatable, but good luck. It's milk and honey. Cowards cling to their shoelaces. Slime slakes their thirst. Crud builds up until the government treads water. Aggressive chest-pounding suckles the

young so that I can assume my rightful place. Deviants roam alleyways on the prowl. The hart's magnetic pull starts to crumble as weed kicks in, and feelers ache for a response, but cholos have stripped the place of its aura. My meters are out of whack. You'll end up trailing behind, fashionably at that, and much changes while you sleep in fear. Regulatory mechanisms require servicing, but how can I shake loose a volley when my mind won't work?

143
What is needed? Bronchitis or carbon dating for protection, upkeep costs, as does neglect. It's a fact. Lives go on, mowing grass, getting divorced, a roller-coaster stock index. Veins of ore temper their criticism, but rationing is imposed, along with an early curfew, and I trip another circuit-breaker. Cheap calls for revolution are in vogue. Salaried employees flip that bitch, as old friends cackle and hoot. Not much else can be done, but it's worth whatever effort. Cold seizes my guts. Namesakes go down in the book, a cult of precision and eternal vengeance. Knock-out genes stress your pumped thighs, their utter aggravation at having been chosen. Reality? Wormwood and gall. In exchange, I exaggerate, but strike three and you're out. The periodic table of elements goes nose and nose. Geese glide over a swamp, pissed at countervailing minds, but Eros can't get any purchase. The answer is no. Don't correct an errant way.

144
Right in the middle an alarm sounds: no more explanation. Gather up your implements. Environmental disaster scenarios max out your account. What a life, devoice of libido and jazz. What about you? Boxing up cast-off goods eats up the remainder, but even that can't shim their frame. I pound in another nail, sparring with the devil for amusement. They Holy See issues its promulgations, although more often than not the pigeons flock and flap around, emptying tills to beat the band.

145
Garbage trucks arrive and depart. Why so many certainties, given unpredictable cloud formations? Within minutes or at most hours you notice unmarked vehicles hauling away hipsters, their subtle agonies ignored or irrelevant if not irritating distractions. Hint hint. Nothing has been moved by even an inch, which starkly portrays impending doom. They've heard it all, and then some. Catheters galore snake across stainless steel trays. MRSA reigns supreme. It's a privilege you won't long enjoy, so stock up. Whose mind is it, anyway? Nerve endings feel entitled because that's how they were raised, so convince me otherwise. Pompous fools abound. Try scarification, for example, or back-room deal-making and fake family relations. Without a shred of guilt you walk away whistling Dixie, and I'm gasping for air in an extensive dust cloud. They are at it again, butchering with glee. Neutrality is a myth as Christians shrink and quake. Your turn. Goofier outcomes have rarely been seen. I'm making a study, sending in teams for initial reconnoiter. A blast furnace goes cold because they forgot about proper embalming practices, but a sharp clear line compensates partially. My jealous arms rage and fall as Jehovah assembles an army. Widows pine. Carnival tents flap in a stiff wind, and plotting grinds on, regardless. Unopened gifts catch your eye, but petechia and ecchymoses tell another tale.

II Local Spread from Contiguous Foci

146
After beauty goes, the cupboard is bare. A ripple appears ever so briefly. Maybe someone else has more wherewithal although rural India floats in the deep. Vegetable love rolls around in its burrow. Timber. Keep your eye on vitals in order to fleece those shills. It could have been worse, which isn't saying anything. Rip out their tongues, or pen them up because, like it or not, ghoulish figures are on their way. I ponder my plight. Waiting nearby gets something in gear, even though I'm hard of hearing. What if they sharpen their blades and hit the ground running? Ethnicity is for sale and commands top dollar, but which particulars were you referring to? Preferences be damned. Curses. It's inappropriate and offensive both, much to their sick delight, and geometry has become obsolete, along with nostrums and snake oil. Clean out your desk. I don't have much of an opinion but would only say the following. Rooting around in a bone yard tests their mettle as human beings, and some come out wanting. Virgin tears regale you in your rubber suit with shades.

147
You laugh until you fall down, convinced about spending money. Putting out feelers stomps their custody battle, and corn is trucked to market. So it goes. A bare minimum exceeds your expectations, rhythmically. That way liars and financial executioners get off scot free, while pure victims are undisturbed. In time I'll arrive there anyway. Calls for pacific acceptance grate on your eardrums. That was important enough to require its own suit of clothes, so don't fight it. Shake that thing. A spring cleaning turns up fallow fields. No more passive yearning for what would feel like a miracle because metrics don't compute. Skip it. You're cranky again, so rattling crockery may help. Bills, bills, bills. Flood waters rise. What is that danger exactly? Random bleeps cross my screen, and in no time you're cooking with gas. I feel desolate.

148
Incidentally, hounds baying generally portends slippage, so if you don't mind I'll continue the exploration although pain accompanies that fantasy. Buoys sway and gong all night. Now I'm geared up, fit as a fiddle. Empty alcohol containers suggest a cultural sea change, but hold on. Maybe it was customary merry-making among saber-rattlers, nothing to write home about. Slowly their transport channels open and close, regulating traffic with stunning simplicity. How can my mind function without pain? Even full membership won't do it, but that's no reason to give up all hope before entering. Halogen lights go out one by one until I'm left in utter darkness, at which point a formal announcement clears matters up once and for all. The rank and file cringe. Don't deny it. Statements about lying become risible, and wolf packs roam about at will, as though masters of the universe. I'm finding it out step by step, a maddening conundrum not to be exceeded. I'll check for leaks later if at all, and St. Peter's basilica echoes with footsteps as the faithful file past, heads bowed in compliance with local practice. Chemotaxis guides the way in a series of linked dockings and embarkations. The sea beckons. Who can resist? Wildflowers paint the canyons of San Diego, arguing their case for immortal beauty before a saturnine bench. Batter up, although curiously in the dead of night. An auditor comes a-calling fully weaponized. Narcissistic sucking stumbles towards its fixed goal, sleep of sorts, ignoring your vicissitudes as is its wont. A two-way street affronts that drive.

149
Now what, another rock pile to be moved for no discernible reason? Check your gauges before lodging a complaint because nine times out of ten a cardio-pulmonary bypass delivers a blow that won't be beat. Exchequer chancellors assemble at the rear since faulty judgment has its implications. No more so-called rules of law need apply. Making do has become a way of life, and the slag factor mans up for a change. Duty calls.

150
Warheads emit a glow. Then I'm back and go down swinging, as the aged detach like autumn leaves in a breathless afternoon. The gathered furies of unavenged wrongs turn in on themselves, and orphans shuffle down tenement hallways wondering what happened, beyond envy, beyond regret. American gas stations year and year. Whose exceptional eyes and hands probe the moribund surroundings, always moving outwards regardless of conditions? A spinning sphere wobbles before toppling, as though accounting for eccentricities were no longer the case, and all that could be hoped for were a few more unobstructed breaths before the fade-out. But no. Sodium runs against a powerful gradient, asserting itself, until osmolality is challenged, which wins in the end, of course. I bear witness in my way. A new day dawns. Rivulets break through. Moses drifts among the bulrushes, and brain natriuretic peptides line themselves upon the cell surface. Where are the little caves or pocks full of lipids? Cascades and tirades plot your ruin. A well coordinated strategy boils them in oil, and down go their guards just as foretold. Ascites gets the upper hand. Watchful waiting stokes your fires, and I exit smiling, subtle as a sledge hammer. Care comes in many forms, so pack quickly before they kick down the door. Jack o' lanterns and hay hooks pepper your memory of a bizarre world tilting towards an abyss.

151
Electricity sways, a hawk on the wing, as those action potentials pencil out to zero. Trash in, gold out. It's a face-off. Colonization peters out. Those with a better idea step forward despite any lingering symptoms. Scaled back projections do it. Mail in your checks. I'm honing in although catch phrases and abbreviated synapses miss by a fraction. The human element wants a goodly share and why not. Dullness descends, as it must, and drunks sleep it off in doorways. Gradual expansion will fill their sad afternoons until even martinis backfire. My bazooka has become an anomaly. An internal pull stabilizes this conjunction temporarily, and a wordless presence tries to make a living.

Another season rolls by in quiet majesty, and the screaming subsides.

152
Impersonators seek employment despite their malfunctioning basement membranes and obsolete leaf-blowers. None of that matters. Consternation flusters their feathers, and I hurry on, dogged by the dark stranger whose embrace I seek and abhor, knowing what awaits in the deepening gloom. Take these insubstantial offerings while you still can because the horrifying machinery grinds on, regardless. Saying no takes precedence. Goofballs get kicked upstairs so that a state of perpetual motion bounces off walls, ping pong madness. I pry an answer loose, but it leads to more work, so pile drivers with donkey engines fire up. Any monitoring will have to be man-handled ex post facto. Advance directives and extreme unction match their profile. Do you want full access, to go all the way in? No Big Bang will bail you out. Details merely distract from a gestalt or warm but untrustworthy feelings.

153
Systemic lupus erythematous runs that number, but renal failure jumps the gun, and off they go. It's a hodgepodge for good old Humpty Dumpty. Strapping lads dawdle while the chop rots. Silence comes on with a cold gleam in its eye, yet I'm nonchalant, not paying heed. Then figures play the foil, filing their nails with elaborately feigned indifference. Why doesn't it translate? The help I need can't be laid out in piles on a grid made of ropes or wire. Will that slake your thirst? I'm so sure. Hematologic evidence overwhelms its load-bearing capacity, and invisible devils torment their prey with sick delight. T cells respond, trailing behind clouds of glory, while a simple Baptist hymn sticks in your throat, something about the River Jordan or meek and mild sheep. A pillow of thistle, dry, cracked feet, ventricular remodeling stand their ground. Neuropathy and bride capture book-end musings, from goddess culture to signal packets. Nothing is nestled in the French Alps, so that a garden path can come to seem positively negative. Who among you carries a

stick? Autonomic signs should be enough although you know how it usually goes. Fund the war at all costs. Apnea or orthopnea, a spiral battles it out for a meat prize, and I wander a flaneur among relics and mater lenses scratched and cast aside. Mustangs take it on the chin, as rolling brown-outs trouble a harassed populace. Now their terror squads sweep up, go off to dine on squid and French fries. I can say that's not my world, but tunnels of love lay that ghost. Help won't be at hand. Old friends peel away as your abused organs move into an end stage. Minor adjustments produce a yield, denuding statistics of their hold.

154
Deriment impediment alone will succeed when oaths of office revert to a babble. Septic shock and sudden cardiac arrest are wrenching reminders, stallions magnetic with raw power. A Maltese cross mashes vegetables, but a toothache can block legislation. Wood chips go unnoticed until shapely fingers compete for loot. I dissolve. Liquid fire flows towards the source. Scavengers observe their various screens, scooping up data for resale. Your compression fracture meets criteria, small consolation for that much pain. A stampede prays politely if possible, and I can't figure out their similarities. No one waits for me. Cartilage shaves it close, asserting itself to make a point.

155
On come billows of night, low blowing thunderheads. I'm full of anguish at this brilliance, as though cut to shreds by spinning blades. A baby crawls on the floor. There is no starry dynamo now that snapped bones interrupt service. Resistors and capacitors are welded in place, strictly ordered through infidelity's laws. Unleashed hormones sear axons. A little dab will do you. Epidermis has a brush with catastrophe, but even a few moments of reclining by the reeds in a cool shade will make up for pathos. It's staring you in the face. Your ruling passion shifts into overdrive, and children listlessly comb through broken furniture and filthy rags looking for food. The government doesn't give a shit. Itself a parody, financial services is hell on wheels. What do they think" Tax evasion trims the gain, leaning

mightily over as I whip along through narrows, then onto a broad expanse. Ah. Put in hours if you want the honey of rare knowledge, while those in need whimper and wail. Each grain is painfully excreted, an equivalence of trash and dreams. A manipulated mystique takes their cash. Hard-headed engineers wonder what's happening, and salt permeates spider webs. Entire colonies replicate overnight. A crystalline lattice branches off, turning the surface into a beautiful filigree. I'm left aghast. Coolness affrights, yet I'm stumped by the very mention, and flaying resumes according to custom. Hairless creatures crawl among dying shrubbery, but field agents and party-goers fight for the last say.

156
Selection of victims proceeds since above all else cozy arrangements form a test case for their instruments. My trapezoid stabs you in rapid succession. Oxygenated blood straddles a divide.

157
Whence these rusted bolts, these bundles of rubber tubing? Genuflection down-shifts into sloth. My self-protection may falter, but have a fresh approach despite countervailing winds, or a torqued political climate. At four the primate will receive you, so check your firearms. Inflamed cells start to come apart in an enzymatic flushing, and old-fashioned teratogenic cross-talk rears its ugly head. Down you go among moist stones where light pales, then flickers out. A theme from Muzio Clemente announces their small entrance, and that quiet terror of sensation shocks your nerves. Don't bother to reroute cabling because they've blocked escape hatches anyway, and further prevarication will land you in hot water. Beyond the shadow of a doubt, I question their motives, as if lawsuits and second trust deed transactions could be avoided.

158
Obsolete body parts atrophy, handicapped by a cataclysmic inertia. What they so pitifully desired turns out to be a dead issue.

Perfect compliance targets their sweet spot, a veritable cornucopia of intransigent pathology. Hotheads with their cockeyed blarney put me off, but dawn brings another conjuncture. I'm languishing in a backwater extracting confessions for a measly living. Right-o. Someone typically abdicates even when half-baked excuses cannot calculate a reasonable outcome. Where is my salvation when I need it, off to the races? Speaking out of turn, they get plastered before wiping up. I get a temporary reprieve. My attempt to fill out a check gets nowhere fast until hairpin curves and dizzying descents. Rush, rush, rush. Oil fills the Gulf of Mexico, and they didn't even have to do anything, so I retreat and regroup. Inferior artillery weakens your already spotty record, but stupidity enjoys a bittersweet triumph.

159
Sidereal shifts roll out over millennia watching bacteria zipping around in their medium. Can you track that flow, a sticky sludge bending and twisting through deep space? Where are the appropriate tears? You got your thousands and could care less. Anyway, the I.C. U. is jammed to the gills. Wing it on a prayer. Valuable ingots slide onto a bloated market, making it worse, while the mellifluous birds of yesteryear croak on in memory. Watershed throws up a defense with its exquisitely attuned guilt about imaginary crimes. Someone has to pay, so it might as well not be the perpetrator, n'est pas? I'm driving a roto-tiller through ancient Greece and loving every minute, even though rude fellows cast aspersions, a broom handle in the spokes.

160
Their cheap sarcasm, a sit come download, grinds itself into any available space. Bloodhounds bay and mewl. Sanitary napkins chart a course of sorts, sentinel nodes pointing the way, even though such knowledge weighs heavy. Come with me into darker corners, and a tearing down lays the groundwork. Who goes there? I palpate my surroundings, the synoptic Gospels calling out in a cave full of echoes. Liquids are shed. Always the allotment returns, a floating dominion that befuddles your

senses. I'm turned a which-a-way. Attendants go about their frightening tasks, a million miles from here. Some malign creature flutters around, waiting for a propitious opening. What is unresolved? Benign positional vertigo floors me, so I grab a bite and hustle. Another generation arises, subsides as waves crash against rocks in their ceaseless and patient rage. My radar blips, as foot traffic goes bonkers. Magnify the process for a fresh, shocking perspective. Somewhere along the line I realize I've passed over, that these daffodils and cheese wheels are time-sensitive.

161

Too late. The Justice Department is caught with its pants down, and each communication bears an ethical load. Homeboys dump their shit before gunning it. A festering culprit stands to lose, so get out while the getting is good. Breakdown products go into a holding tank, and I sob openly because why not. Nit-picking nitwits revel in their own stink and filth, but that dog won't hunt. No sense in going that route. Split the difference so as to keep things in balance. But beware. The shallows will do you in. Suppurating orifices drive a hard bargain, something a child would know little about. Terrifying loneliness squeezes my bones until I scream. Maggots feed tenderly, while the ploughman sweats and tramples clods. Take my vomit, these polypeptides that never made it. I've thought of you, despite any evidence, and again am submerged in my own pain. A glass wall provides qualified respite. At 6 I'm confused because changes are not observable except after a long absence. My, my. Look at you. In vitro fertilization trains assiduously, or some religious anachronism panics when they fire their howitzers. In the name of an angry god they assembled devices and negate mothers' milk, as though a tape recording of animal noises might contain a key to the mysteries. Error multiplies, whereas virtue goes into remission. Blindfolded and trussed up, I pan the scene. Selfish arrogance ponders before leaping. A bearded lady has learned to sleep because that frontage road gets on your good side. Logic choppers distort my pathogenesis, yet somehow a strange attractor arises, and water runs uphill, to my surprise. What is mutative, to coin a phrase?

162
Spectacular, extraordinary love affairs are reported in the news, and a leveling off begins. Imagining pathways extends an olive branch, nothing more, nothing less. You laugh. Instead, fold up your blankets because foul play is suspected, for example, strong-arm robbery. At least I don't have to invoke some abstract mystical horseshit to back a naked power grab. They ease into their prescribed roles. Once in a blue moon I see the heavenly city, with its spires and crenellations, banners flying gaily to announce an imperial event. But dire plots threaten their connubial bliss. It shatters, running off in a confusing medley of disparate concerns. What spoof lurks in the mauve shadows? The ace of pentacles turns up unexpectedly, and I'm marked forever after. Your accomplices give you away. Duly noted. Dew forms on rose petals, runs crookedly down amongst thorns. Reports of assault clog the media as janitors and maids keep at it, their violet eyes downcast and ready. Eventually, I give up. Who wouldn't? What if I mentioned the whole story? Unfractionated heparin flips a bitch, a real howler putting them in stitches.

163
Who puts images in your brain, throwing cascades of chemical switches, millions of proton pumps? Once it starts, a force whips you straight through, and bingo. Daredevils and wallflowers mix in gay abandon. My namesake boils in oil, having destroyed three generations and counting. Alpha Centauri backs its play with real money, not whistling Dixie. Always something. Stalking horses, you might say, but who gets cheesecake and who doesn't? Blended families spew forth their seed right from the Book of Psalms. My helpmate selects an appropriate switch. Instant results would be desirable, but your chosen standard-bearer has called in sick, although nickeled and dimed by petty bureaucrats. Dare I admit it?

164
Come level on average, their maintenance contracts have lapsed alongside insurance riders and evolving genomic monsters. Well, yes and no, come to think of it. They're going in full-bore while my Clostridium species takes up residence for a launching pad. Apoptosis presides with haughty disdain over a massive skating rink, and then some. Where goeth the wounded healer in absentia, in flagrante? The master of the hunt pulls no punches, and Oxford is a pile of stones whose narrative has become less and less seditious, so hike up your gaiters and move out. Gas gangrene or full-on caseating necrosis pins its hopes on a star, even though the caissons have ground to a halt. Vegetable status comes as a thundering relief after inadequate life histories and forged wills. Not even a thief in t he night could have done better. I examine denominations incised in flesh and granite. No one calls. Children have vanished, and my feet move slowly through fallen leaves. They have issued their seasonal mandate, sick to death of provisos.

165
Suicide launches its fleet of black galleons under an iron-plated sky. Sadists gurgle, and your skin crawls. Nothing is as it seems, but sinewy grasping after one more quantum tears apart my fascia in the desperate attempt. Do you doubt it? Whose identifying marks will be posted now that old-fashioned shoe leather is steeling itself against the torrent? Formaldehyde and ginger ale violate fixed precepts. Then death dreams rear, so that I wake up panting, confused. What has become of me? Electro-chemical chain reactions make deposits and withdrawals, not as stiff and robotic, which is reserved for more personal attacks. Deaf musicians tune their instruments, and parched throats strain after moisture. Thee is no let-up. Cow dung and potassium leakage are just the ticket, hellions without a doubt, or scholars sneaking around with nibs. The ostrich gains purchase or at a minimum averts igniting a fuse, and homemade bombs decompose in the desert sands.

166
Destitute, I sink lower, until cheesy smiles fade, and sad winds knock around the shutters. A few stolen moments gnaw greedily at their tare. Down here among sightless crustaceans I eke out an angle. C-section statistics revel in that belated realization of essential goodness, worshipping at the altar of crass materialism. Human growth factor and erythropoietin cross swords, but an upper-cut equals lights out. Emotional signaling tolls a knell, despite statins until acidosis overpowers the security apparatus. Not that it matters. The whole rickety shebang lumbers on, like it or not.

167
Lance lowered, I charge toward a cliff edge. Sometimes they can't or won't deliver, so I pick up a blunt instrument with serrated intent. No effort is spared because you can smell rain in advance, and thugs grab their Louisville sluggers. Shadows huddle together, quietly weeping so as not to disturb the powerful and entitled grandees. Hundreds of thousands of prostates can't be wrong. I file it away, confident of nothing any longer now that they have destroyed another coastline. Ambulances arrive and depart as though staged by expert opinion or focus groups, by fits and starts coughing and burping out their contents. I hover nearby. Charged ions flip-flop like grease-ball politicians or sociopaths studying their prey. Please press the pound sign before punching out, or your mortgage will kill you. Lots happen, but bucking up troops isn't on that list. Wait and see. They have breached a supposedly impregnable barrier, weapons at the ready. Coma ensues, abrogating the love feast or jousting tourney. Vacuoles and other organelles go hog wild. My mind bounds, snaps back, loses the scent. I sink into a trough that almost blots out any blue. It's cloud cuckoo land even though that hangar has been vacated. Air brakes do their doggone best, by crackie, by gum. Lead poisoning creeps up on you.

168
Certifiable. Merchants of suffering tally their take for the day. A stern taskmaster reverts to type, and after-burners kick in. I'm

always tired. Spider-webs festoon the rafters. They ate themselves to death, as though fundamental limitations of time and space didn't apply. I go on, dried sand crunching underfoot. I'm in a wind tunnel, zooming towards the white window. One by one they fall away, permission to exist retracted. Unfettered carnage has a way of bringing down the house, despite that phone call. Sarcastic grimaces underscore their gruesome demise. Gains slip away. I stare off blankly contemplating nothing in particular. At length an engine looms up, searchlights ablaze, but what about the insect world, celebrities of a dim kingdom? Death is in the air, full of wailing and gnashing. That's when it hit me. Listen to their whispering because someone's pharyngitis will smoke out your opposition. A senseless wooden demeanor administers automatic and mechanical blows. Sperm counts and carnival roustabouts edge out the competition, traders in living systems regulated by a membrane, basement or attic. As luck would have it, whether tarred and feathered or merely left to perish, I perceive thinning brush that gives way to an unexpected expanse of delta. Silt deposits structure several civilizations, yet it's never enough. A longing for love goes unmet. How else could you look at it, given those years of brainwashing? Partners in crime collide on the dance floor. I don't know what to do, fractally. Pain floods the alluvial plain, and pangs spur me on.

169
Someone has to submit to Ananke amidst the cold anguish of late spring doings. After an eternity of inexcusable delays, documents appear, and rancid clothing fires back its caustic response. Stains remain until they go unnoticed, but which ones get to shine? A vast river sweeps along, ignorant of even its own history. Savages sniff about, and a full moon dangles itself beguilingly. Trollers purposely blur the field, as a stunning silence precedes their definitive defeat. What pulls you through, an identity as part of the mineral kingdom? Metabolic alkalosis throws in a monkey wrench. After-shocks go on for months, but my pretty little ones hardly notice as they burrow and loll. Constipation runs up a flag, and terror camps click in. The need to feel trumps another chess victory, and irregular extrusions dot that surface, in the process

creating a complicated landscape of declivities, valley, or dells, and gentle rises, perfect for eyries and lookout towers. You do it without an after-thought while the Dow Jones index lurches like a drunken whore. Rates of change fall under my limit of perception so that the golden section, despite a certain theoretical sanctity, explains very little. Oil traps those dynamic flows, until tired fee yield, go into yaw. Foul gases bubble up, coating their bodies with a precipitate. Tight tolerances float your boat over even as a malignant demand attacks re-bar and I-beams.

170
Input doesn't match through-put because an enzyme pathway slips in the possibility of multiple energy packets, diploid or haploid. Who controls? A singer of note comes stomping up the stairs, and professional consultation raises the roof. Going unacknowledged fits that bill. Falsies and blind alleys add their two cents, diminishing accounts. A contract or close shave explodes, raining clock parts across the abused city. God has spoken. Neurons want to wipe the hard drive, as if an intravenous line could take five with relative or absolute impunity. It's a straw man, because they won't be regulated in the interest of time. Plans change. Sweat pours out in frantic preparation for a dance of veils. Their Disneyland conception of government fills nail holes with putty, hamstringing one more civilization with snow cones and ear buds.

171
Pay warrants and cigarette butts enter that well-oiled shredder, quite a la mode, and check it out. Factor X down-regulates your life force, a thankless chore. Let them mop up later. I'm grinding uphill, blowing from the effort, and freed slaves don't bounce right back. Agents train their weapons on unsuspecting passersby. Deep in a dead mind the broken peptide chains cast about, lacking their previous confidence. Aldosterone launches its skiffs, and troubled waters bode no good. Fighting and yammering burst my skull open. Strangulation victims sink underwater soon to be forgotten despite volunteerism and a

deprived family background. Crusting seals that deal. Cyanide and the whole spectrum of acids slip into appropriate boxes on the chart, but weak-kneed opponents still can't strap down their vanishing species. Instead, they arm the air. Figurative formulations help slightly, but come on. Utter immobility sets a stage. Anxiously you keep scanning a scarred horizon as though seeing the bullet would eliminate all pain. They laugh at any destruction of human beings, especially those shot at night. Nothing can be done, because overpowering force stitches up the very wounds it inflicts. Anguish is not exaggeration. A rear-guard action strains your resources, but that's the idea, a one-way ticket to paradise. See? Fishermen are coated with salt and tears. Nary a word is breathed, and hunters' lore dies out fast. What's left, a dried carapace, some casings, the nacreous sheen of shell innards?

172
You think? Cheetahs huff and they puff, while captaincies are doled out like parsonages of old. That reek is a dead give-away. Without having cultivated the white folds and hedgerows, you still expect a windfall, salad days. The cries of early morning gulls wring me out. Electric lines stop at the desert's edge, where I stand gazing out over a sandy waste, having come this far. I buy my watch and wallet, not caring about any noise. Journal pages blacken in the flames. Each step leaves a hole. You slide, thrown off your stride, across a web of absences and pointless keening. All this and more, much more. Trigeminal neuropathy obliterates those notions, and there is no apple cart. Old photographs crumble away as seasons roll over them like breakers with their eternal yearning. Roses blooms, and you begin to feel that pinch. A vanquished life hunkers down for the duration, and painful memories abandon the field. Without realizing it, I wander through thickets of ink and fiber.

173
I'm poised near moving water. Over there a fly-covered carcass rots away, and the authorities seem unconcerned. I'm afraid to check for identifying marks, a boar's scar or superficial flesh

wound. Everything slides left a notch, nauseating me. Lesions appear out of nowhere, hungry as wolves. My figurines and magical objects constitute a dike. I tend to my small fire and go on sharpening stakes. Shatter-proof glass explodes into a shearing dust, as rose quartz stores those emotions removed with a cold-knife procedure. Radio-ablation chomps at the bit. Their transceivers are tuned to a dead channel because that ilk cannot conceive otherwise. I'm rolling around among cables and clipped leads, feeling for a female part, but gun-ships and commando teams square off, raising their dukes. I smell offal, loam, industrial chemicals, burnt grasses along a county road.

174
Your swan song has gone sour. A widow huddles amongst charcoal and damp bitterness. Vespers ring hollow. The muezzin falters in step with incipient molecular uncertainty. All suggestions are rebuffed, understandably. Take what's in my mind even though nightmares and anaphylactic shock eat their way through family histories. Who were they? What could they have wanted? Testicular cancer is no more prevalent. A paralyzing shame stops them in both directions because signaling goes in reverse. I'm concealed effectively behind a sheet of flames, nullifying an infinitely hateful world. Reactive oxygen species storm a citadel and reduce it to rubble because ligands are off by one bond. Use caution. High voltage. Gliomas sprout like spring joy. Your face says it all. Money and shit dribble out as if revealing secret strings of code. You have to understand. None of this is planned. Only ions get through that cameo from Pompeii, and a capacity to do nothing but contemplate an imagined end, some anxious loosening of the grip. Will a star burst in deep space beyond a strung-out wormhole? Hard science bricks up that tomb, and metaphors wobble before tumbling. At a fulcrum, I pull through a block of threads. Afterwards, your drive demands its due, but disclosures of such details, although devoid of feeling, are just as exacting, if not persnickety. I suspect someone is there and fear it is so because of grueling tears at night. I would have lived differently. Homicide statistics blend with nitrogen and helminthes in an upchuck. The rumble is on. Bigwigs and

honchos make no bones. What am I not seeing afloat amidst particulate matter, lodestone or thermostat? Impulsively I thrash about, as someone gently knocks. Trust" The psychotic core springs into a blur.

175
What binds the pieces, a commonality of plight or spirit? Sense shrinks, cutting the hawsers, and fog thickens when you least expect it. Allowances will no longer be made. Rest assured. Only a handful pierces that gloom searching for a fibrillation profile. I plump pillows to postpone evening's iron claw. Databases change hands in a dance of shadows against ditch-banks and full-fledged officialdom. Pedophilia or hemophilia, add your surcharge and be done with it. Hyperlipidemia masks carbon offsets until casual flings swing into full view. Gravitas sucks a big one, along with anhedonia and orchiectomies. Bilateral. Before there were so many, green and gold held court. I no longer stroll but allow myself to be distracted just in case.

176
Here they come in their institutional whites, weighed down with instrumentation and protective jargon. I know my turn is around the corner. Eye contact cannot be avoided so cut back on carbs and stop obsessing. Fickle hearts lack fundamental decency. Top dollar goes out the window and down the shitter. My fantasy inclusion of necessity absorbs its own brutal limit, endocytosis and undoing, but how can this be? My beaten mind boggles. An object that never was can't be lost, and simple enumeration drives that one home. No skin. Bronchiectasis, calcium channel blockers, obituary lists intimate otherwise despite dignity. Phagocytes fire up. I assemble a cast and assign roles but end up wincing anyway. Double-click and see what happens. Colonel so-ands-o moves pawns around, feeling for advantage. A dicey proposition banks on it, but bit by bit their grand scheme unravels. An old acquaintance hands me sunglasses, as though trying to get rid of them, and I step carefully down a narrow path along the water's edge. When was it every any different? Another huge loss looms. Words fail, even as morning light wages its

eternal warfare. An arrow points downwards at an angle, but if you're observant maybe those incisions will offer up fit sacrifice. A stoical visage messes with me to counter their boondoggles, their hot-air balloons. Astringent measures move through committee in a forced march to the sea.

177
Where do body parts go? Confidentiality dictates a maximum of six minutes before alarms sound. Deadbolts rust as I feel around amongst bent nails, twisted hinges, bed springs. Adjust your rheostat accordingly but only well within contracted parameters because some clever engineer broke that hex and in so doing levied a curse. Horse lather foams and drips. A cool million stares you in your baby blues, so whatever you do, don't out your innards. Meek and mild victims expose their necks to a blade. I know it well despite that phony nomenclature. Heart-rending cries cannot quell that angry outflow of black poison. I'm stumped. Cadmium yellow leaves show up their pitiful opposition, and weird deities bowl with thunderheads. Attrition decimates the ranks. Downstream, depth charges crunch numbers, but why rush it? Nothing occurs, a bramble patch of pain for your trouble. Smells of light gun oil and fried onions qualify. I am the recipient. Please take a seat. Stragglers are shot, pure and simple. Description leads off, hankering for its own brand of intimacy. Courts of love take root, with their adversaries and opponents. A bower bends over graying temples, but how far out must I extend my reach? Control centers are going on stand-by. Set phasers to stun. Endometriosis cashes out and longs for stronger drink. Even after all these decades the horror endures. A purple heritage will throw you off for sure, but I'm not that brave and pull back. Lethargy spreads its tentacles. Your juvenilia is on the chopping block, and anyway tree-top views encourage a more profound amnesia replete with disturbing syndromes.

178
Whose thermostat could stem that rage? I've been at it for a lifetime, sifting through curd, flathead screws, rhododendron, wild rides across New Mexico. They must pretend they are

machines fresh off an assembly line, an army of robots with shit for brains. Gases sweep and swirl, going against inertia as blood follows that gradient faithfully, and I slowly come to understand what I never was able to before, that the vascular tree slinks away. Both fists slam and pummel, delivering a coup. Loneliness drives a wedge, setting loose a deluge before I disappear. It's the only way. A pall settles over the meadows, and frightened pleasure-seekers scamper off before a chilly wind. Perspiring shirt-circuits out. Straightforward confrontation does the trick, but don't count your chickens because right and wrong take turns. Shame is the name of that game, and look how well they play, puppet masters par excellence.

179
How can I ever be reconstituted, with a missing chassis? Please hang in until fruit drops. It's not even necessary to say anything. Gradually a torture chamber emerges, a sickening ignorance, and my feet and legs turn to water. An ape-like mask swims into view as galleries of onlookers gape and snicker. At length they retract their pincers and send me out into the world when the real fun begins. Of course I'm fat and ugly. How could it be otherwise? Indian snake charmers and mongoose handlers keep that pot boiling. Drunken collapses into uncontrolled sobbing add their dollop, knocking up a divot. Ten million reactions later, nothing substantial has in fact changed, but the machinery grinds out its own version regardless of what you may think. I'm surrounded, and there are no reinforcements. My explanation falls on deaf ears, or waves of data sort themselves variously. Royalty are stripped of their cherished titles and thrown out to starve. A malignant sun scolds the asphalt, impervious to entreaty. Does that count? Ravaged scavengers scour the landfill, and furiously barking mastiffs make their point, plowing profits back in. Nothing quick clicks, because cheap cynicism displays its true colors. Rubies and emeralds abound, nicely evading theological jargon, or is it merely debased gibberish, gobbledygook? Messianic drum beats echo in your head despite best efforts to block that punt, with aplomb. Whether simplex or duplex, faulty logic fans those flames, and no bluebirds fly. Intimate

descriptions burn up the road. Hammerhead sharks dart and wheel. Afterwards, love will triumph over all. French fries and ketchup round out a delightful menu.

180
Medical necessity and quality assurance review roll out their big guns although I know something. It's buried deep beneath a giant oak. Gracious hosts extend a palm branch. Let me be absolutely clear. Cognoscenti exit right. You mouth your customary platitudes, and petite mal seizures shut down Wernicke's zone, or is it Broca's? A reduced scale renders your visions futile. You call them fungible assets? Panic looms, and cockroaches. Frijoles in a splatter pattern clue you in. Gonorrhea would have been preferable, but choices were slim, and the storm god was angry again. I bow to the gale's wild force. Darkness comes on. Rock and roll wrecks your party.

181
Quick-draw artists have surprise on their side. Fuck all answering machines, and fuck voice mail. It's filed away for posterior. Some horse-faced quack is pushing pills a dime a dozen, but I'm not in the mood. Cryosurgery and radiation postpone the horror, but think positive. Johnny One Note goes ballistic because watered down wine is better. Deal with it, that is, if you have to go down fighting. Your heart is a firing pin, and armor-piercing rounds wallop the shit out of them. Now you see. I haul in stones, millions of necrotized cells stacked in circular rows to create a crater of slush. Why go on? Spontaneous bruising heralds vascular events on an unprecedented scale. Germ cells jockey for position. They are packing up their paraphernalia, circus rides, the big top. Beef stroganoff and Chianti, sex on the floor, a mournful gaze over rows of headstones, and that's a wrap. Warped minds distort and torque to a cusp and beyond. Fear of pain goads me on. Dour dowagers decorate their expansive verandas, and I hear clip-clopping of carriage animals. My systems verification monitors never sleep. A soft tread escapes words as large wondrous eyes tremble on the verge or brink. Nimble fingers look to the future, that nebulous zone of carnage,

but whack jobs redress old grievances as though brought up on charges. That's what you get for a few hundred dollars. Pharmaceutical policy overrides random outbreaks, clusters of illness in a star pattern. Clerks pore over parchments by candlelight in open violation of strict house rules. A fetus doesn't make it on through, and marriage offers no guarantees.

182

Mutual recognition among common strumpets wards off their mumbo jumbo. Westward ho the wagons, despite zephyrs and scorpions, and I begin final preparations. Something gets driven into my hippocampus. Deep sorrow cooks in an alembic or beaker, and anxious alarums are sounded. That parallel process flaps its lips, begging to be taken care of in old age. You tell me, because my sight reaches only so far, and the last witness has conveniently fallen off a cliff while on vacation in Hawaii. Straight out of Hollywood. They talk but say nothing. Poison-tipped darts do their subtle damage, closing circle after circle. Dust clouds shift slightly, and I catch a glimpse of a pockmarked urchin feeding on misery. Human shoes capture that spirit even more than the feet they protected. You do you stint, then pull up stakes and light out. Chaff, chum for barracuda. Nothing is more lovely. An alphabet of objects takes shape just after each green flash. Fog hangs low, grumbling among bushes. I follow any available branch or wire despite entanglements, which reminds me. Don't get hitched, even if they have the gall to invite themselves.

183

It passes away, crushing underfoot your proud constructions. Dancers leap and cavort in open revolt, while pathogens find their way. Now your little tricks don't cut it. Abdominal pain scrapes away any leavings so that your undivided concentration can go for the gold. Gee whiz. Gyroscopes and nautical instrumentation cram in a shit ton of data before formal remarks, ceremonial back-slapping, and good Havana cigars. An astrolabe would have helped. Sobbing in the dark underscores your plight as sad-eyed janitors push their carts down deserted hallways, across marble-floored lobbies. A blank slate invokes matrimonial customs, hard-scrabble faces used to penury and trivialization. Diesel fumes and streetcars accumulate at each intersection, stamping their inevitability into the built world. I melt in the heat, recombinant gene splicing despite peptide bonds. There you go, shooting from the hip as though heroes and damsels had to punch out at 5 just like line workers. I crack open these shells. Dental impressions make every reasonable effort to stage a given illness, but even whining serves weird purposes in that economy of give and take.

184
Downwind the river smells portend invasion. I'm genuinely moved, but guess what? Foul-mouthed instigators double down despite house odds. Fabric dealers roll up their bolts because the time for shadowing has passed. I see the obvious with lockjaw eyes. Data strings fill an invisible traffic jam of competing harangues, spilling their invective and delusive ministrations. I'm slamming these walls with balled fists, bug-eyed, hunted for sport. Guardians sharpen their tools and get into position. Ready, aim, fire. Interdigitation is held in place solely by an unseen network, and congenital slips in where chains are snipped show up much later. Maybe it's thrombocytopenia or agammaglobulinemia, but idle breezes stir roadside trash as I lie here quietly so as to take a series of readings. I keep telling myself it can't happen even as I know full well otherwise. Carnal desire fries in the flames fed by chunks of fat and charcoal. A disturbed spirit is abroad. The crow gargles nails as random machinery demands attention. At a fixed hour shutters come down, and furtive glances retreat further into a lonely familiar zone. What was I unclear about? The pain becomes unbearable, and then I go dead again. Blasting caps hem and haw, stigmatizing your face at point-blank range. Shame orchestrates a resurrection because row after row of numbers stretch to a hazy horizon. Chisels complete the picture, overcome with yearning that is never to be satisfied. Meanwhile, their magisterium multiplies, and clay fills their mouths.

185
The Golgi apparatus cranks away bent upon its secret ends, despite howlers in the macro-process. Angels lock in bits and bore through muck, all part of a day's work. For a minimal buy-in you walk away with cold cash and diamonds, having ignored obvious clues. Storms blow out over a surging sea. At compline you hear only distant doves because it's going away in a long sigh. I'm there on the other side somehow impaired although still able to wield an axe. What would it be like, some imaginary alignment between good and evil, say, or a pit bull on a rampage? Valences, emotions, tics stammer out their glue or marred curves. That's the deal. Stalks or coins fall. No blame. Tact whether adequate or exquisite stands to lose its legitimacy, but a ride back will set things to rights. My mother is hunched in the kitchen corner with a knife, as night winds thrash the salt cedars. Ropes become chains. Page after page feeds that loop, and the forms of giants rise up in an enantiodromia, hungry to adjust the thermostat. Any expansion brings suffering. Wounded beasts howl and groan, but the Almighty reaches out sublimely for nail clippers, the keyboard, a corn dog. That's what corporate wants, so suck it up for starters. Give a shout-out. What a hoot and a holler. After they breach the defenses, they colonize and spread. Those who relapse go under, sure as shooting. Nociceptors fire away. Living beings require refuse disposal, which is where I come in. Antediluvian monsters prowl through stock philosophical conundrums until the cows come home. Take your ticket and wait your turn along with monks, convicts, and teetotalers. I figure someone else must push on through a wall of spit, banking on the best enzymes. One more car accident or Bar Mitzvah and it's a jinx.

186
In a jiffy you're gone. Lessons learned and forgotten haunt the grounds. Weird enthusiasms sweep northeastern states as snake handlers and sword swallowers train their sights on a better tomorrow. I reposition my radar disk so as to cover a wider swath of sky. There is no other time. Rats establish their appropriate domain, and I'm fending off pesky invaders. Gears within wheels

sicken me despite non-steroidal anti-inflammatory drugs. Flying robots pinch their earlobes for luck because the world as known and loved is doomed by the superior entropic forces of stupidity. I can't. Isis wields pinking shears. Notice and register goes that comforting refrain since no one escapes one last gong, not even gung-ho journeymen. Space empties out so that mRNA can kick-start a race of morons. What a waste, sniffles and all. This report conveys only a few essentials. For a comprehensive account, consult your local timetables and narcissistic aggrandizement. Carbon deposits are sealed in amber beneath multiple atmospheres of pressure. Bear with me. Dogged insistence ruins your chances, and riding bareback splits the difference. I hand over my mind and have it trashed. Everyone is complicit. Illogical dicta tip that balance, but aching bones make their peace with the shovel. It's fruitless to differ.

187
A pilot light burns on and on even though dopamine reserves have been exhausted. Impetigo or carbuncles, it's a matter of S. aureus. Galvanic skin responses couldn't have put it better, but cellular memory makes a second shot either more or less likely to take, depending. Help will arrive, but panning for gold steals a march behind enemy lines. Once again blood flows, as elder statesmen belch discretely in postprandial satisfaction. Who could make this up? Frame by frame a cosmology takes form. I stretch out my arms beseechingly, but all the good ones are taken. No more separations guaranteed or your money back, now that an agenda has been set. You go in for a scan, only to rack up rhetorical questions. Frigid conditions talk the lingo, and latching on comes to seem abnormal although it isn't. Baroceptors signal a change. Incoming flights are experiencing delays, due to conditions. On a monthly basis it works out to insolvency. Having given up, I merge with the dregs.

188
They specialize in refined forms of cruelty and take an idiot pride in their own viciousness. The Queen says so, while beating horses with wire. At fixed intervals a buzzer goes off, and pellets drop

through an aperture into liquid. You absorb a dialectical blow, your mind focused on the hunt despite systemic expungement. Everyone is running amok. Gentle chiding has no place but takes an arrow from its quiver. Light pushes through, trampling age underfoot. I'm at war. Knotted scar tissue abbreviates motion, and fantasies of unfettered selection come to grief. Refueling hits a snag. Then what? Off come the gloves. Short-fiber twitch equals a gelding. I don't know why but note periodic pandemics or if omega-3 fatty acids merited full disclosure whereas lifetime awards are in cold storage. No sloucher, that one. You can't trust metaphors. At least let's be honest here. Desperate felons shoot themselves in the foot, which goes a long way. Nothing here is even worth stealing. A gate swings back, smashing into the wall, and I no longer imagine an intact mind taking it all in. Instead, old masterpieces fracture along geologic fault lines. Small symmetrical piles of bone dust are digitalized and disappear back into ether. The jig is up. Deep-vein thrombosis is the least of your worries. The lovely ones who soften edges aren't exactly part of the package.

189
A hodgepodge rushes pell-mell over the cliff. Viral flare-ups establish hegemony with manifest ease, old hat. Much has gone wrong in my clinging to words as if courteous confirmation were a patent crime. Noblesse oblige or common sweat checks its holsters at the door, and I retract quickly to avoid attack. Think on it. My isolation chamber stalls out on an incline so that only sadness and panic remain.

190
Shell out, or get out. An edge of nausea forms, as I total my pitiful plunder. Tinnitus deafens me to your sales pitch, but some structure of breathing supersedes tales, imperatives, and strands are clipped and capped with telomeres. Be real, and flush it. A grand recapitulation leaks news among the narcotic blabber in bars and committee rooms. You haven't an inkling, and neither do the have-nots. Barbed wire goes for broke or anyway a song. Whether recumbent or prostrate mollycoddles the bottomless

pit. Once articulation falters, then fondling begins, and who knew? They are up for grabs. Central processing units choke off data streams heavy with age yet lacking dignity because of all that derision. I hear a gravelly voice telling me stories about princesses and bees. A trap door snaps shut, over and over. Tag. You're it. Blast-off is at 0700 E.S.T. Picklocks and garbage handlers allow themselves to be put into strait jackets because of loaded weapons and ham-hock fists. If you don't roll over, a whistle blower or turncoat can't be held to accounts since tattletales are drawn and quartered. Just smuggle your bullion into a safe house. Knuckles become purple.

191
Swarms swirl around and through me, everything imaginable in a coating of gray. There has been no touch, therefore, no beatings. What do they expect? You look for evidence of yourself but miss civic watchdogs and the renin-angiotensin-aldosterone regulatory loop. Present arms. Little thought goes into that one because a subtle wave-like action detracts from any logical targets within striking distance. Lapidary, I absolve you of all responsibility so that you can bull on through. The mess hall is to your left. Subarachnoid hemorrhage jimmies that door right off its dumb-assed hinges, and whose debrided larynx gets credit? It does matter although make sure to check your exact counts before coming to a provisional formulation. Better yet, scotch that one. I'm heaping it on because like begets like until an outbreak of virulence scorches the earth, and dead fowl fall from the air. All praise to your ruler. The emptying proceeds. A great lamentation goes up as I pick my way among corpses and orange peelings. This they left, fodder for magpies. Such touching innocence, since despite those years sometimes I can gaze across flat rooftops without vomiting. The key card slots perfectly, but to what end? There is nowhere else. Kindness seems dilatory, oddly out of kilter. But carefully drawn documents are of little assurance, either, so I revert to type. False leads gobble up your slim margin.

192
Doomsday shuts down your experiment. I have qualms so I quibble and prevaricate. But hyper-arousal and chronic inflammation eventually collide midstream, creating a vortex or dust cloud that darkens the day. Engineering feats scatter their offerings at your feet, as though humble. How about that? Nominal changes track their pained confessions of incompetence and foolhardy impulsive outbursts. If you can buy, why rent? Stalwart swordsmen man the ramparts before demanding the ultimate sacrifice, to put it mildly, because come August their last recourse will be to flee. Cobwebs cover those cornices, and a long march awaits. It's a provisional operation, dilation and curettage. Absolute ease of macular degeneration is a game-changer, but malar rash and mild joint pain implicate the capsid layer. I'm juggling timetables for a bored and spoiled audience whose meat demands overflow with dead neutrophils. These are certain. Septicemia and tachycardia rack up points as though there were no tomorrow. Wrinkled brows furrow further because warmongers can't get enough, ever. I see a visionary elk with large wings appear among trees and move cautiously towards me. It becomes a woman straining out of her leather bra. Weaponry and savagery recede. Something else awaits me, but I'm sidetracked by ten-penny nails, scree, the capillary bed. Who sets the hypothetical end-point? Judges brush their teeth before gaveling away a life or two. Gosh, really? Gee. Hey.

193
A reassuring finality accompanies their travel plans now that waterways and lost souls figure in as bit players, back-stage Johnnies. Where did those formerly compelling desires go? You get another shot before they pack it in, a cold resignation that brooks no opposition. Once and future bishops drive off at dusk for dinner engagements while their confused acolytes wonder about pay chits and meal tickets, to name a few. Signatures stamped and notarized are required, so take it on faith because massive stores are grinding me down. Lactation does its thing, a marvel to behold despite limited gearing. Dismay unattended spits out vituperations and imprecations to hamstring the enemy,

but neither craft nor guile puts food on that table. Consequently, I have to go back in, fangs bared. In these troubling times only bold moves have any hope of hitting a homer. Veils and shadows deepen as I'm pinched and jabbed, fit object for a campaign. Paper pushers step gingerly in quicksand. Where is the havoc you're afraid you wreaked? Each is immersed in a pool of silent sleep. Stingy shits hoard their holdings for a future that can never come, and porters while away their off hours playing whist and jawboning about the war, of all things. I'm winging it, pricing rice in China on a breath and a prayer before inducing out and out narcolepsy. The coal chute is a real eye-opener because famous murder scenes magnetize an unbelieving public. What do they care? No accord is reached, so quiet waters among green grasses presage their untimely demise as actors fit to be reckoned with. In fact, vaunted powers of observation renege on their promises. My distilled bitterness keeps the home fires burning, and calculated repetitions are not the end of the world. If there is one, pump that stomach back into the Stone Age when a man was a man. I'm fried, but that's no excuse. Word gets around, the be all and end all. You have to wonder, what with their chattering and puling. It's a standing ovation, an open invitation. Endometriosis gums up the works.

194

Subtle flattery erodes your face cell by cell until trance workers have their chance. I pull myself back from that prospect and its verve and brio. Who is on parole here? Electrolytes and metabolites pile up, soaking in alcohol so as to extend their reach beyond their grasp. Blame who you will, worms turn soil while impossible odds face down utopian fantasies and death-bed confessions. Where's the bite or sting? A black widow goes severely about its business, no longer enamored of the free and easy doings of yore. Instead, triumphant funeral parlors grin about dignity and comfort as farm implements covered with dried mud bake in the summer heat. But wait. Call the number on your screen. Toilet training tills that ground, turning up clods while coolly removed clouds terrify the compliant clocks. Population projections growl and snap but enjoy only a sad, hollow victory, because I'm passing into an inner chamber after my endless wanderings. First, however, the choicest cuts god own the drain so as to allay debilitating anxieties. For good or for ill, I'm filching trash to fashion something of that ilk. No streetwalkers or cat burglars drift into questionable practices despite a trove of fenced product. Man the decks, because a knock-down drag-out looms and lists dangerously. Nylon gaskets are bound to splinter. But clinical trials push through a genome, and revenge fuels a take-over. Credit limits rock and roll. Loyalty frays, and along with it food stamps. Substantial losses mark the mercury as wankers strip for action.

195
Contrition drives in its cruel spike as I studiously avoid strings of beads, ball bearings, bushings, grease-packed U joints. Small talk balances books for a fee as I scamper out of range, rubber-necking like a hayseed on Fifth Avenue. Old contacts go away, as leaves turn, then fall gracefully into oblivion. Angioplasties hover in the wings licking their chops. Almost but not quite, I'm out and about unbeknownst to the powers that be. Stack your washers and bolts carefully because of the life you save. Your teeter totter is broken, and that's the nitty-gritty. Heave ho. Marionettes fire up their song and dance, salted away in memory banks for eventual delectation. I'm in my wooden tower with an over and under and a bolt-action both. It's taken care of, so if you will add your John Hancock on the dotted line. Monkeys clamber up a rigging, bearers of bad tidings while I plop down in dismay because you're hiding behind your answering machine. Who are these shadowy figures that appear around the edges? Safety in numbers doesn't play well despite industry claims, so I practice a coup-de-grace while keeping my other foot on the brakes. Regimentation lays groundwork for colostomy procedures, sad to say. Formal entertaining takes place elsewhere, and rabies throws a wrench on my foot. There is no progress except through haphazard pathology. Maintaining currency? Forget your abused cells that tremble in a sightless world. Hard cash calls the shots. I'm gazing, waiting. Tomorrow will bring its exertions, cool winds. My desire for constancy goes unmet other than by these

palms and vines, but voices unravel, leaving a monotone of love and terror.

196
Hard facts and soft targets take their marbles and leave. Tumor suppression factors go against the grain. Adjuvant therapy hits its high notes, and winos lurch and reel, addle-pated. I lay out my goods on a cloth, whereas career politicians seize the upper hand. Talk about disorganization, lack of human contacts, and the cost of neglect. Then it's too late for old coots. I notice the familiar taste of salt. Why? Whichever pathway gets activated, yellowed sheets are stirred by a listless wind. Mild regret trickles down rocks and among loose gravel. It's a going-out-of-business sale, so take a number and wait your turn. Someone has to be stupid in the scheme of things. Phagocytosis casts its net far and wide, but that won't affect your automatic transmission. Life has other plans. Basic needs, for example, sketch out a strategy for invading the capitol despite carcinogens and mutagens. Once in a blue moon haggard witches plumb the depths, but temperature extremes box in a spread. A direct line no longer exists despite wishing and hoping. I fall back, assessing damages and eager to launch an insidious strike, but please. Their spin cycle hits a wall. When viewed from behind, or the inside, which this is, everything looks different. Pediatric insolence throws in the towel, and little ones go begging, along with perpetrators of their suffering. Archaic expressions fish around for something suitable and come up empty-handed no matter how sure-footed. Aneuploidy. A mish-mash of outdoors lore can't help but turn it all into one big howler. Apply liberally, and sit back. If you must know, electronic disruption is part and parcel, so dig deep into muck and mire.

197
I'm pouring gasoline on wounds in preparation. Pneumatic drills bore through with ease, and droplets form as if by magic just prior to a general conflagration. My glycemic index pulls the ripcord. Panurge slips off between tree trunks, snickering. Multiple rounds bear that brunt, taking umbrage by the book, by

Jove. Halitosis and fallen arches configure your awkward departure, but substance abuse ignites after-burners. Cowards bite their tongues. I'm bitch—slapping senators, but those needs artificially inflate raw sewage without any surcharge other than a fiber-optic cable. States rights take a tumble. Whole banks of switches flip their lids. Famine curses the land, and the dreary seasons crank on in their grooves.

198
This all got started way back when. I had to memorize word lists in order to hatch a construction process, and magnetic guidance systems got rechanneled. Droves of cattle plod towards their chutes. Surging waves announce definite intention, although not fast enough. Husbandry is recommendable if ultimately insufficient because of numbers and coefficients, not to say quadratic equations themselves, those precursors of what will remain. Molecules are mapped. Quarterly inventory stuffs gaping holes. What a cheeky bastard when you stop and consider, but who's counting? Adolescent whipsawing portends a bail-out. Go down into a sulcis for your answer, but don't expect to emerge unscathed. I should know. Sidereal advance listens to the unconscious, fruit of many failed transactions duly recorded, then discarded. I soon learned not to matter. Otitis media is recruited, whereas my vascular tree goes straight towards aneurysm. Shear stress batters the opposition, and nitric oxide or natural killer cells are under the gun. Where is the risk? I bore them, clearly. Once there, it won't go away. Crawling in shame I look down, concupiscence of the eyes. No one would guess, because I've pulled back my turnkey instructions. Everything goes to a null grade, as it's deriment impediment. Making the grade is coupled with backsliding. Ancillary articles of incorporation eat away at your fundament, and I move at will through eateries, passages between tenements, smoky cellar warrens and along riverside footpaths that lead beneath iron bridges. Who conceived this chaos of wrecked cars and abandoned steel mills? The absolute logic of things glistens, thinly veiling a putrid mouth oozing its maggots of words. I snap to. Any desire to push on is sapped, so that when news arrives

from the front no one notices. Give them the brush-off, and look for the ramrod. Lard-asses dredge up their sludge for another leptin-fueled go-round.

199
The protagonist got lost because stop-gap measures fell flat and air ran out, yet one can hope. I lie in bed wondering about many things. Bulldozers push garbage into a pit as words turn to poison in my mouth. Here they come again with their hypodermic needles and panic attacks because of the eternal war. Endocrine uproar alters set points so that the ship's gyroscope goes out of whack. Generous to a fault, the master program resorts to its redundancy just in case, and which life-cycle segment will perdure? Each is worse than the last.

200
Vibratory waves pass through underground caverns. Output targets and productivity curves drain chemicals from the atmosphere, yet what about edema? You enter at any of a variety of points because toggling changes nothing since morning fog is indistinguishable. Black bile and corpuscles compound that fracture. I'm sobbing through my mouth pieces. Action absorbs blow after blow along a continuum until distant horns announce night vessels. Nothing else is different, which I now see with shocking clarity, not that that makes it so. The concrete and steel beams rage on mutely, and sad skies bear silent witness. It's closing time. Malignant cultures expand their reach, dying for more carbohydrates. No sense in adding to the befuddlement. Dog eat dog. I await spiders, hawks on an updraft, root rot. At least that much grapples with the odds, but virions hunt for ligands in a lost world immune to nostalgia. Really? Benchmarks are lacking, of course, so galactic drift up-ends those laws as trapeze artists do their thing, even though with a disarming pretense of nonchalance. What can you gather and report, now that xenophobes are emboldened if not inflamed? I'm building a little city. This is what has to be, the deep horror of who I am, lightning flashes across an angry sky. Recidivism takes a plunge, and a deluge of data wipes the slate clean. I've chosen not to

immerse my central processing unit, but other forces are afoot. No sooner named than obsolete, they must nevertheless submit to hacksaws and assorted tenderizers. Emotions somehow never got developed, so how could others exist? How could I?

201
The arrow of time is notched. Grandiose and swollen with serum, you pluck a thorn, until pain nerves kick open the gateway. I see their backs and arms covered with tattoos, a bonus. A tutelary spirit presides over festivities as I set up shop in a gene pool. My fortress is impregnable in its very looseness, made up of plaster and sheets of plywood. Forgiveness is denied despite its fairly recent invention. Trauma returns full-force, a dust storm deep in my gullet. In this regulated way I maintain contact because otherwise I go under. I'll accept their petty syntax but no more. Corner kiosks float away unbolted and brimming with enthusiasm, shedding viruses galore. Texas hold 'em sweeps the brain-dead planet done to perfection over a bed of coals. One type blends into the next, and you can't trust your senses under the circumstances because warriors have replaced killers. Physical revulsion merits a modicum, wouldn't you say? As I proceed with the fiscal summary, gross outflows deplete your coffers and exchequers. Meanwhile, more children starve. An animal wants to operate their pile-drivers, but grease and myocardial infarcts show up in compressed ratios, while haughty socialites lap up resources. Their little squirts provide welcome comic relief and all will be revealed in good time. Somehow I'm not reassured, because male and female created he them, as if that feedback circuit did not exist. I'm scratching at a barrier. White noise has mounted an offensive. Squadrons to the fore. Day in, day out , k known felons prowl alleyways and fight off nosocomial infections, but ineptly.

202
Excavation proceeds, even though veins have petered out. I'm removing individual grains of sand at a snail's pace because conversation comes at a price beyond my reach. Something resembling bird sounds pierces a circumambient fluff, and

chained slaves don't know what to do. The structures of thought are installed nightly, whereas voice adjustments adapt or die, according to natural law. Phase them out. Histrionic fireworks bedazzle the weary masses, all the while planting dark seeds. I go my separate way, entering obscure haunts with growing dread. Identity is beside the point here, or claims on birthright, air, and food. Flight plans appear in dreams, and a launch sequence is initiated gleefully. There isn't quite enough oxygen, hours later, to assure the bleating herds. Guardians of the book of names are laughed offstage. Vaudeville triumphs with its tomfoolery. Match point, after which drinks at 6 for the best imitators. Fire in a ring of stones won't do much, but their gilt-edged securities burn just as brightly, and no more so. Souls flow back in to unwilling rock.

203
I'm always in the middle, tuning instruments. To be in a permanent questioning state nibbles at the latest oil slick until you remove your name an i.d. number. Cave dwellers waste their brains on engineering problems while thieves and monks gather for solace in a storm. A series of ideas forms, and each worker takes a nail gun. Common household products are stacked up for demolition, alongside old Bibles and bleach in jugs. Check your epidemiological projections because the desire to help masks a philosophical impasse. Gross systems rest on their laurels, but a science of lying meets their needs. Fibromyalgia and phantom limbs split the difference, or haven't you heard? I roll out ropes of dough never before suspected, yet muscular object relations sneak around trying not to be noticed. Mt. Everest awaits the heart-broken, the crestfallen. Faked bank cards work wonders. Billions of cells can't be wrong, so that fractal organization ends up explaining away any discrepancies in the facts. I'm licensed to kill. Anubis and Set strut their stuff, hogging the limelight. All rise for cold hypocrisy that needs trappings, lacking a dynamo. Where, oh where can they be? Lockdown. Battle lines are drawn but can't be relied upon since day one. Giant molars grind up that wharf, leaving an empty lot. My soul turns to steam and escapes through louvers, but the news cycle burns barns for fun and profit. Scrimping weighs in, awash in fungal infection. Just a

smattering but more than enough to torque the odds, I keep them close on an off-chance. May I? By all means. An industrial smog spreads to the hamlets and mini-malls as in days of yore, in frank violation of decorum. Which reminds me. Instantaneous signaling is revolting despite the peasantry and their fleas. Just this case, or all conceivable cases, there's the rub. Microscopic evidence stumps them every time, but don't count your chickens because I smell a fish.

204
Fish or fowl, you name it, as long as regulation play readies their engines. All fall down Mental schemas flicker and flash, fade. A jolt sends them packing. I plane down surfaces, depending, but cost-conscious consumers slip past the hammer, anvil and stirrup. One more trite blueprint shaves points, and comfort equals stasis, at which juncture I pull back my chips. Emergency rations erode confidence, but that's how it goes, a series of troubling vibrations. Dime-store heroes have a moment before subsiding into longer slogs. Basic trust goes out the window, and who's left? Don't dare look up from your intricacies. Flash points multiply like crazy. Mealy-mouthed politicos stand by. Write finis. Alarm chirps and tour guides throw in together so that level-headed thinkers can open up a can. Nope. Give me the straight dope. Brutality and aesthetic pleasure don that garb, but gabardine is out this year. Veneer counts. Plush seats push back because clowns also have bank accounts, and a sonata or fugue bites. Trial separations, whether square pegs or round holes, scratch that surface. I trot them out, ready, willing, and able, but sick and tired of boondoggles. Maybe a court marshal would turn the tide, although blunt-force trauma rakes in coin. Trumpets and cymbals greet their maker, and elephants sway along like gray galleons. Which vectors will prevail? Sedentary beasts go to pot. Naturally enough, the coagulation cascade goes awry, and posses rush off in all directions. A madman concocts revenge beneath the water level, until a hysterectomy kills that fantasy in one fell swoop. Etruscan ruins bear fruit, on the other hand, so that equatorial heat waves are nipped in the bud.

III Direct Inoculation after Trauma, Invasive Procedures, or Surgery

205

No more preparations. 500-foot waves wash ashore, so I have to take an alternate route. They want to be someone else, caught in landslides of cosmetics and liquid crystal displays. I wait, breathing calmly. The sphere of silence takes control, but alien voices blare their tunes but get no credit. Little animal sounds comfort me with milk. What will germinate among this rubbish and sheer teratology? It comes from within. Their bitter soup sticks in the mouth, and orphans make up their minds because they have to. I look for any pretext, licking my wounds. Who is that there in the mottled mirror, on a bench strewn with fast-food wrappers, kicking through leaves damp from late afternoon rain? An old face dips and sways to adapt to corn husks of autumn, sorry for wastage and cowardice, but the prow cuts through. My demands go unheard so of course unanswered, and animal tracks disturb the sandy graves. I'm arranging coat-hangers on a wooden rod, desperate to see some order before coagulation or toxic shock so as to justify as if this were a shabby county courthouse. You want to turn thinking into doing but feel rip currents. Go to your nearest command post and await word. Speed matters most. Jugglers and mountebanks round out a roster of high jinx, slapstick antics galore. Westward ho the wagons over a knife-sharp edge. You won't get any further under, because of special effects now executed upon a prior digital platform. That, too, rushes into a veritable maelstrom, and your genealogical tree becomes driftwood to decorate dying beaches.

206

Up and at 'em. Mayhem has its own laws, although unwritten to date. Flamboyant stone shows what they are capable of. F-16s thunder away, violent and sad in their proud isolation. Who gets to be the weakest? Whose grease gun is the culprit? Winds knock down power lines and billboards while the electorate sleeps, ignorant of their own complicity. Desire languishes under a hostile sun. Then come wild schemes, hot-air balloons that dot a scabrous sky. Ignite and run. Revelations of abuse wrangle a deal, but pearly whites plead out. An unconscious predation inches up on blithe spirits. They pander, but it can't hinder improper allusions. Jackals dip coupons and while away a lazy day. Absolution may be provided but only to the worst offenders because recreation of those benign circumstances conduces to an end stop. Childhood prevents decay. So what? You have a choice, and the cold fluctuations of moods receive an order. As you were. Glorious martyrdom knuckles under. They gave me a shellacking, and I extend wary feelers so as to disappear from sight. Arborescent, excessive vines push deeper into the empyrean, and scabs form automatically. Is cash acceptable I want to be with your forever, but breeding rules intervene. They are hanging fire. The consular officer mucks it up as I disassemble electric eyes. Behind scrims I proceed. Obesity makes a splash. A parade of prancers keeps them in stitches, and 200 feet below you see clear, still water stony in its patience. Self-effacement becomes a tad aggressive when the chips are down. Without approved referents, doggerel substitutes for clear thinking, and botched attempts lead down a garden path to the cliff. Check your file. Illicit gains push out quality, adding to their haul.

207
Confusion reigns supreme because of lost hours and the gross national product. How does it feel? In a manner of speaking, that dog won't hunt. Concussion vomiting likes to flaunt its knowledge before unleashing howitzers. Hair burns first. Don't try to pull a switcheroo on me. Wishing won't make it so, but janitorial services might. Dream on. Medium heat does it, so pick and choose now that dollar days are here. Give that idiot a wedgie.

208
How would one go about such matters, once accorded such short shrift? Reasonable paranoia strikes out, and my memories dribble out, evaporating, Madrid streetcars, say, or an entire world of insubstantial images bolted to a needle. Faces flicker and do that shimmy. What if? You wouldn't even know it was happening, so

to all intents. Don't go there. Business days rack them up, a landslide defeat, verbal homeopathic inoculation. Well, well, well. Close, but not cigar. Nudged or shoved, my pinpoint iron sights are jostled just enough, whole homing devices malfunction. Lifelong struggles with cloud cuckoo land finally man up. Why this pride of ownership tour? Touchy, touchy. A orange glow spreads through dust in a quiet, filthy world. Obligatory family visits mash your nerves. Bruxism pulverizes our last shot even as you sleep, because chiaroscuro angles for a leg up, as the crow flies, never from point A to point B Each mission has bendable rules. It's noticeable somehow even if as a carom. Despite unclearness their tanks punch through, now on a rampage. Nightingales and red-tailed hawks go to town, to your chagrin, if not worse. Historic highs revert as if on command, and legal beagles bungle it badly. I bury that hatchet in a soft midriff. The crowned heads of Europe haggle over pennies now that bung plugs have been popped. Another story unfolds to divert before divulging, and warts or wens will wiggle free. Stainless steel houses vegetation, so let the hunt begin in earnest. Old gray-beards bore them silly with their nattering drone. My voice box is full of sand and rusty nails. My refusal to know shields a nest of dead fledglings.

209
In far-flung reaches I fish for pieces of eight as if adrift yet under assault. Gross vehicular manslaughter compounds charges unimaginably until a kind of dam gives way in the mind. I'm disposable, apparently, because carnival carriages with parti-colored pennants sweep by oblivious, and I study dust patterns left on waxy leaves, or how rain trickles down panes left exposed along coastal byways. Local gods have a ritual of shit and praise. Oxygen and enzymes come roaring in on asteroids. Proof positive. Cleverness kicks a latch support, and my dedication leads in a circle. British pounds sterling goad their raw flanks. IgM gives them the royal bird for starters. Caloric parameters must match a master plan, or gadzooks and egads. The pony express gains momentary traction, and vesicles release their toxins in a cycle of boom and bust. Steroids to the rescue.

Bonding of goods stabs my soul because who owns what anyway? Fetishism is a tip-off, as though procuring your heart's desire in its sick wish for love, and it's guaranteed for life. Dead brains pile up. They pull out micrometers so as to gauge basement membrane as lumen width, a caliber of concentration and expertise. Gobs. A shit ton. Jealous eyes flare and flame, but peace becomes an obsession, one well worth its weight. Sample descriptions leave out the grist or gleanings Destiny has a way, and Islamic archetypes seize them in their slumbers. Dial it down. Vaults bleed out in a hemorrhagic fever. Parry the thrust with your perfect matriarchy, until identity cards are demanded because they return to their base under pressure. I hear crows in an eternal war with air and sunlight. Merlin presides over a hierarchy of holding companies and offshore shadows, as dermatitis does its dance of a thousand veils. Pay attention to that shifting texture, smooth plastic strips that repel curiosity.

210

You step into prearranged chromosomes, none of which you created. Building permits are strictly controlled, but lapses in oversight scuff the image Priests file in, obedient and passive. A cult classic assumes its rightful position among a constellation. Corn gods verify my epistemological status as gyri and sulci expand and contract or herniate through the notch. At long last their fixed scales are righted, even if only for the nonce, but long enough for me to stagger towards a traumatic consequence. Subarachnoid hematoma unpacks a crate of mirrors as ocean-going vessels disembark, hungering for information overload. Enter your PIN for a printed receipt, while fantasy crowds roar their approval. I'm not around that long My wings were clipped, mainly out of ignorance, and the regular pounding of corpuscles weakens endothelium, until I'm eclipsed. Losers take a beating, bolted down securely against all comers, but I digress. Dark vapors rise and mingle as framing of liver enzyme readings shifts leftwards, and bulwarks begin to swell. Gravity straps one on. I look back and notice I've left the machine age. In fact, topical creams and unguents play right along, but yelling and threats have no place As if. The Czech Republic erects one last monument before hammering its swords. In a laptop unreliable thuds portend gloom, and I doze off, struck down by a horizon. Within summer's tender shoots little good inheres. Slowpokes and cowhands fashion a utensil stained with dried serum. The law's long arm dismisses individual differences, human nuance, until thrashed and left for dead. At least their bankrupt narrative turns its back as wires fall like flies. Corruption creeps in, hallowed by tradition wherever it pops up, and precious little initiative rises to the top. But grease accumulates as if long-range missiles and crush wounds had to respond to rude demands. Any lesser amount goes to the wall. Sputtering lips cashier their hopes Basalt obelisks line various grand approaches until I rally my forces for another go-round. Broca pipes a fresh new tune. It's picture-perfect although down at the heels. Snapshots of the ruins take on a patina, but universal? Check guns at the door. Recompense figures in, of course, but whose iron lady goes on the block first?

211
You note miniscule changes and question their veracity. Antelope mating habits test your memory of the good old days and find it wanting because gold standards stink. Get it? No time for small talk. Handouts mock kith and kin. One's vision comes back around, crazed by the heat so that delusions retreat until a more propitious hour. Despite combing the hinterlands for magnets or trace elements, Bible manufacturers haven't yielded an inch and, in point of fact, are taking on water. Then I go back behind the veil because so much gets concealed in revealing. Confetti bedazzles mute crowds as though fine-tuned receives had not lost a signal. Lunacy and water damage conspire against a moribund federal bureaucracy. Bomb bays open as those same old black-magic facts are drearily rehearsed. Ah, the sweet smell of new toys, a simulcast in ten languages flattens history beneath a firewall. I take my stand, shaking a puny fist against the onslaught. A dirge troubles rhododendrons yet I plant pittosporum undulatum trees as though time meant nothing. Please report suspicious behavior because a biological wheel turns. No need to fear. Cough syrup and NSTEMIs furtively

unravel the knotted sleeve of care. Weirdos smack their lips because of crash dummies and hogwash. Insurance turns ugly. Aggravating, that no sensitive abraded soul whines about things going away. Commissioned musicians must pipe that tune or go hungry. What chicken wire binds those tricky truths? A persona imposes cocktail hour, just to be seen even if only in a flash.

212
Nothing begets nothing. Stern faces float out of a mist or low-lying cloud. Poverty seeks its own level, and coadjutors do their ever-loving thing. Spinal shock and stenotic events conspire in dream time. A walrus mustache completes the image. Stray curs root through garbage as I bow out, making amends for past infractions. If you slip, you're screwed. Water seeps under carpeting, and their horses rush off madly. Raucous drunken laughter rockets down hallways made of sheet rock. How did I end up here, after so many wishbones and sharpening stones? What do they care? Sleep becomes irrelevant, or so states my obsolete manual. Excess gets skimmed off, and who is the wiser? The light softens, and I recall a street in Lugano. A berry aneurysm files charges, as though sad streetlights burned with a piercing nostalgia for places never before seen. Until then, I'll rein myself in, keeping half an eye out It's archetypal. Otherwise, why bother? Packaging caulks affected seams, that is, predictable blast patterns, whether solely somatic or not. Rapid response rates drill right through, and lickety-split you're there. They deliver another stinging rebuke, but salivary glands have had it. Humidity runs down the walls, and you buckle. Scrambled eggs pull a fast one, although I'm just saying. Hydrostatic pressure requires a quick fix But hard-core headaches and inflammation of meninges flip their flags to spell out added poundage. An aging infrastructure heaves with sadness and delay. Quicker than a wink, uploading a downlink presses flesh, as I evacuate holding tanks while maintaining the pretense. Work details ensue puffed up with their own importance, but pride goeth before. Attention to detail becomes evident, just not why. Ringing never stops, even for a breather, but then shy should it? Secret calculi vie for an icky prize. Pride of accomplishment goes up in a cloud of

smoke. A chilling effect descends. View now, or view later. You can smell it in a voice tone or particular posture, well within parameters. Constant illnesses create a rhythm of micro-organisms doing what they seem to want.

213
Chicanery and snookering mold a compliant herd. Factory orders spin out of control, decide to go national. Coeds and tech start-ups burn bright, then fizzle. Movement levies a tax and angry rain batters fantasies to shreds. Oxygen saturation loves to play the fool. Cash flow is contingent on thunderheads, a wish to lie down among grasses, to be done with it. Each one has a different story, if alloys can be prepared for eventual, eagerly awaited jobs. Call the question. Dormant beings abide peacefully, and I brood and fret to no good end. The hilt runs with gore. Incessant travel defeats the purpose, but stage fright freezes you in your tracks. They have designs upon their neighbors' fortunes, a running battle with gimlet-eyed destiny. What could seem stranger? A glaring receptionist paws through files to keep up appearances, while outside you'll see nothing but pine barrens and gray-yellow sand. Take the local if you have a choice because that way lies Samsara. Zealots have overrun the agora. How can the body be left behind, and should it even be? Ants make their way across the corpus callosum, blindly believing. A haunting melody lingers because of prior commitments. Flush with recent successes, they count their blessings and turn to strong drink for much needed solace during these trying times. Trigeminal neuralgia leaves on good terms. Dead-end retail plants its standards. After all is said and done, go back to square one. Bunch of piss-ants. A trellis of ramifying latticework creeps out by night, and sick revenge fantasies hack away at thick rock. Fearful little creatures wouldn't last a second. In such straits I look for push-overs. Fond wishes clog drains, and a whiff of corruption sets my hackles on edge. The entire outhouse of culture grovels because practice is lover. Why equivocate further when annual reports buckle? The sea rolls on, inevitable, cold.

214
I make final adjustments to a failure to thrive. White noise masks clandestine operations in stodgy prose and gooey sludge. A dove lulls me until bottom-feeders move in for the kill. Boring tools are ready to hand, and clocks strike their puny hours full of their own importance. Strangers ride mournfully into town, looking for respite. Identical twins? An orange perches atop. How much can anyone take? My heart is a meat-grinder. Photographs lead a parallel existence, as if muscle memory were all it would take. Nothing pans out, yet they blabber on, ripped up by a cheap laugh track. Co-morbidities and pharmaceutical big shots dance the night away. One way or another, a vanishing act upstages your limelight, and dreary amusement parks stumble and gasp on through summer blight. Respect gets lost in a financial shuffle. Away goes a train of thought, as though San Pedro were on the moon. Innocent victims line up docilely. An empty landscape stymies my effort to pick an apple as I watch control panels for any blinking lights. The sphere shrinks a few more notches. Delicate butchers know those ropes, and each chance, no matter how slim, loosens a slip-knot. I'm tuning a receiver. In some ways, nothing has changed. Chain-link, weathered boards, dirt. A 20-car pile-up slides in sideways, and fraud stalks the land. Choreographers of hell sip tea while personifying evolutionary trends, but squalor and lice string them up in obloquy. Mass hysteria assumes a position, and centralized services want for naught. To go on I have to stop. Nerve roots permeate another kingdom, as far as I know. Getting and keeping, a hypnotic gesture kneads you until aggressive screaming destroys memories against a backdrop of gunfire and waltzing. When you lose your marbles, toting iron makes the grade. Thousands are drowned with more to come. Gadflies and muckrakers rejoice, but don't alter their sacrosanct liturgy because who does that deed better if not the archon? How little you see. Quiet violence completes its mission. Nothing excellent remains. Persimmons detach, fall straight down. One's chosen path clamps shut spring-loaded jaws. Down-shifting costs me, in blood. Ah, the complexities.

215
Which alternate route takes the trouble? Flaps of flesh say it all, but a safe full of documents with that rated capacity passes with flying colors. Skin makes an impression, superior by a long shot. In order to be on the up and up, I revise my thinking because courts of law troll dark waters. Regret spins itself out, wistfully. Now they can't say no since I've gone over that edge. Letters of informed consent wash away in late summer floods. It bodes ill, and assassins of fantasy lick their chops. I see galleons groaning with booty, a fata morgana realer than real, but whose tired wisdom prevails once you start making exceptions? They are all gone but one or two tied in knots by their mutual love. Bio-markers signal ischemia, but why sweat it when zippers will burst? Cartoon characters fill their mouths with sawdust. How about that? Concrete pylons line street after street, lost in an endless videogame. Checking averages yields only short-term relief because of dermatitis and gas gangrene. You get something for nothing and seem unaware, but your gullet accepts whatever comes out of the chute. Brown hillsides stump passersby, and land-locked farmers stare stolidly at an unforgiving sky. Trust dilates when possible. Victory goes to the berserk, even if such animals manifest retinopathy. Radar screens light up, delirious with happiness. Access routes are crawling with cops so I'm donning a clone, an outfit beyond their reach. Parodies undergo shock treatment even though jugglers and harlequins ad lib with their facial hair because barricades can't stem these rambunctious tides. Jobs are scarce. As haunting tunes saturate your flesh, osteomyelitis can't hold a candle up. Adios to Mother Nature, and don't look back. Apolipoproteins lose their exquisite tuning. I flow into that niche, scanning for threats. Moneybags goes it alone, but knowledge of procedure cannot blend with suburbia. The lacquered boat pulls out on another journey of forty rounds. Theme and variation lay down that groove, a fosse or blood trench. My daughter plants a tree.

216
Enter the narthex and gaze lovingly at a source. Coring out granite blocks assembles a human vision, yet your omentum swells ever onwards to its apotheosis.

217
I am alone, awaiting pain. Ropes of care tear at my guts. Outside, all seems calm. Upheavals do not alter windows, paint, even the smell of old pine and car exhaust. Sociopathic warriors work for their flashes of feeling, dependent on evacuation and power-washing. Your Red Sea runneth over, or whether an invitation awaits can't tip that balance, so suck it up. A whirlwind of placebos and overtime chits taunts you with your very life. Insurance games extinguish a row of torches, and rank asserts itself almost contemptuously. Then I'm spared until wind walkers stride out with great confidence. Who carves that branch when hands lift their pitiful tools against a gathering gale? You're in for a caning. It's the drugs, regardless of thrones and principalities. Some inebriated architect designs a plaza with a fountain pool full of broken glass. Listen: a call to prayer. They speculate openly but find magnetic fields nevertheless. Tears flow, a litmus test for ancient wrongs. Continents continue to drift, and there is not time for dreaming anyway. Those who dally mix it up and charge more. That whole cannot be filled. Don't doctor your data because clutter will out. I find myself wishing for truth serum although frying pans and colic cannot reduce the quagmire. Respect assumes a very weird form indeed so that doubters come to distrust their own pneumatic brakes. Just as well. My conscience won't let me, even if the best ones are under lock and key. Their sheep have been purloined, and joint tenancy may feel right but their cancellation rate packs a punch. At vespers you'll notice bats. Somehow nerve fails at a turning point or fantail. Crowds father for a lynching but otherwise can't be drummed up because air and smoke carry a sad tune. Controlled access severs ties. Any productive labor will be subject to mockery and chronic misrepresentation. Drug abuse hamstrings their talent, and manual dexterity slips up. All that work for nothing.

218
They come and go according to an occult rhythm, dead in the water. Who has enough balls? Ignominy pursues you, a harpy of sharp accusation. An open refrigerator door knocks back and forth in a slight panting breeze. Knowledgeable workers pass on love before they assume that mantle. Lust beats the piss out of them, one and all. Genetic irregularities make mincemeat. I'm whipsawed by data flow and deep threat of summary dissolution. Body sounds and miscegenation stretch webbing between guy wires to ensnare night beasts. Supposedly helpful hands are extended, but country justice milks them dry. I'm raring to go but ill-served by dint of force or character. The floor shakes. Cottontails scamper to safety. It's diagnostic of something more severe, an inability that forms a crust I can't see through. Why hold on so ferociously when the tide is receding? Blank stares emerge, disturbing a studied calm, and you draw a single conclusion. Multimillionaires can't help themselves, caught up in a zephyr. That date is booked, after careful evaluation. One-way streets time departure to overlap with a well-worked vein, so I stand ready, receiving whatever they dish out Chest-pounding stops that clock, and reasonable considerations ignite another powder keg. You might think of subcultures or random affiliations, but what could be worse? Water runs through my fingers, as I reach after phantoms. Charades rebel. When resignation sets in, cachexia stalks its victims despite repeated signals. Fake smiles give away that game. How else is it supposed to be? You go the length and then some, but what of it? One bad rap deserves another, even if annual check-ups go unheeded. Earthquake insurance wangles a deal. Reliable by-products decompose along with whatever metabolites. Leaves scatter before the raw wind of history. Smells of ice-plant and dog shit take and take until the control panel blows a gasket. Whose version, or which, comes to matter less, whereas lamebrains and wild boar extinguish desire in its very accomplishment. In the fullness of time shots are fired, and nameless figures from a forgotten era clutch their identities greedily.

219
What do I have to give, held back by geological deposits? Masterful strokes create form in the bruised mind. Too old, I accept twilight and a foreign language. No bicycles come rolling up and alcohol coats their sphincters. A tender farewell ushers in pain and longing. Rash actions let off steam, my lowered eyes carefully obedient. If only nocturnal dysphagia would let up, I could score that surface more deeply and at least stick it to them, your point being? Churlish oafs bumble through simple chores, steadfastly refusing to grasp basics. Hack my way in. Electronics experts fiddle with controls, compulsively rushing about, one step ahead of catastrophe, or so they are persuaded while disconnected laugh tracks rattle on in schizoid irrelevance. Nevertheless, the sun comes up, then goes down in an absolute order as though multiple crime scenes were of no significance whatsoever. Mirrors face one another. An enactment staggers under its load, while gulls scream and wheel, passing within inches. An asteroid seeks its prey, as I study another set of shadows. Cool concrete collects pine needles, even though walkers want their foulness to be overlooked. So many years have come and gone that a smile over the shoulder freaks you out. Relentless self-criticism ensues because property tax gouges much deeper. Finer than that they don't make them, so search no more. What a panoply. Accessible funds distribute their stench, while I plot out scavenger routes. How did I get here? Chance operations string you along, despite obvious dissatisfaction and entitlement. Of course you expect a free ride since paying denotes conscription, if not cruel fate. A blade falls at the hour. Legs move in unison, and sleep sweetly beckons. Someone answers, none too happy with parking arrangements, but bumper stickers go no further. An atmosphere of accusation ruins things. Subtle digs undermine escape tunnels, but which benchmarks will count once these fires burn themselves out? Old family pain pollutes the ground water. Excuses and fabrications roll off their tongues.

220
Downhill ski buffs keep a hand in. What do they have in common, now that rank collusion is exposed? Once a week isn't enough, so expect a cooling trend. Look how easy it becomes to slide because the mind plays fast and loose with its infinite possibilities. I recall a particular beach on Mykonos, a boat coming in for fresh vegetables. You duplicate yourself for mass distribution, yet that pull won't let up. Popular culture sticks in your craw, and my battle strategy comes unraveled. Rain smells fill whatever so-called space remains until I again reach my limit. Strike soon, or live to regret expanses of silence. Shame has its say, as usual, and forgetting is a blessing. Trash pickers enter the fray, driven by a chromosomal storm. Then I return to a common scene: chair, rug, books. Dredging proceeds. A woodland sylph coughs. My sickness draws a veil over itself, but vapors escape, and the parable told by dead skin and sagging flesh wills itself out of the picture. I, too, am a robot, a worker in wood and air. Now that an inventory of reflections has been completed, I can walk confidently towards the black. Persistent scanning for heat stamps becomes a protective measure, and they are squandering their patrimony. With each successive generation coffers churn. Wild animals melt into a benign tapestry of evergreens, much as these summer whirlwinds. It's a holding tank. Others have that word, and the former peaceable kingdom seeks converts. Pistol-whipping as an art form advances in those rankings as cranial sutures move into place, not that I matter in the least. Danger lies everywhere, fulminant. Hinges creak, or is it a bolt? Hypotension advances despite countervailing currents. Neurological deficits bloom, and colorful analogies filter down even though police action stalls out in a pickle.

221
Put it on pause. Silver is extracted and sold, but I don't understand how they can issue commands so automatically when twenty million are homeless. International cooperation hangs by a thread, and coolies perform furtive exorcisms by the book. Each one is trapped in a mind. Acidosis stays within its range, no matter how many times I repeat, pounding in connections among

billions of links. Why is it all necessary At an anguished juncture the train jogs off, and in no time you're alone by cooling tracks, listening for any signs of life. Youthful dreams splice wires bb they storm the battlements. Take no prisoners. Frontal assaults box themselves in, and superior tactics carry the day even though the paradigm sucks. No evidence is found at that scene or anywhere else, but some authority issues a ruling so it doesn't matter. I decide to name names, pure and simple. An old pattern persists. Howitzers are traded in for peripheral neuropathy and diplopia. I hear ambulance sirens. The metabolic syndrome appears out of nowhere. Maturation proceeds despite cortisol and carbohydrates. Soon. Meanwhile I wolf down forms and orders from on high. The smell of bandages grates because irrigation practices are written down nowhere, so sleep intervenes. Magnesium overload works that vein. Shallow thoughts enter the lists, and anxiolytics burrow into spare change. A ticking time bomb changes channels for kicks. Officialdom smirks with self-satisfaction, but you'll have to hustle. Sojourners seek respite among mysteries. Who can blame them? Floaters dot the waters, and I cash it in, or only in fantasyland? Fatsos lumber along, down-regulating themselves towards a bleak afternoon.

222
Solo. Mass culture gets in line. Menstruation and air travel protect basic incest taboos. Psychotic refusal burns a hole right through. That's its power. Now what, a mewling? Beyond that age you're screwed. Flesh melts off under the impact. Any further deposition adds fuel, naturally enough, but modesty contains an explosive charge, a pulsatile rhythm best suited for delivery. Now I'm collecting. Shields are cast down. Square roots and quadratic coefficients need help. What are you bringing? Let go for once, caught up in a perverse universe. Deference cloaked as courtesy inserts a dirk, and the youngsters go on cavorting and chortling. Stir-crazy, I place my offering carefully. Echoes die away killed off by insurance. A stake or post destroys dreams, and Europeans find new ways to attack themselves, invigorated by bright blood and early morning bread. Being criticized, therefore, I rack up

hard-earned points. Small victories shrink, and I'm upside down, foraging. Emotionally, another matter. Hemorrhage abbreviates its formal address, getting down to business whereas starvation and scoliosis repeat a plea for clemency. Surprisingly, inflexible front lines repel invaders so that one more day of horror can leak away in dollops of plasma. Slinging hash keeps away the wolf, but for how long, and why, given long-range objectives? I inflate, then collapse in a sad heap, desirous of revenge but incapable. Drainage tubes run a risk. Wanton or not, I'm over-exposed and busy setting up guideposts that won't be seen for generations, a strange preoccupation. Resignation marks triumph over mere sweat and that rationale for entertainment, but what is the distraction from? Somewhere among their heirlooms a fully functional appendage rears its head for a look-see. How can I deny my nature? Self-regulation doesn't always pan out and pluripotent cells send out scouts for scoping.

223
Word gets around, as rumor has it. Ditch those bitches for an honest go-round. Justice delayed goes into remission. You take what you can get. Fighter pilots eject. The dermatome tells where. Despite appearances, nothing is random. Brains study themselves, as though in defeat, and spiders crawl among brown grasses. Return for a full refund. Vanity and destruction tick off their winnings because in this way maybe swimmers will slip through. That alien nomenclature makes its demands. My job is to provide for a full registration. To do so, I attend, caring but as if not. Their old victim plea, with tears, of course, carries the day. Adapt or die, sooner. Priestly ministrations come bearing gifts, but graveyards and petunia beds receive a dark bounty. These appointments take on a luster although brute force itself succumbs. Look who decides. Scorpions do their little dance, and I move on through blackness no longer housed in special quarters. You glide among ramifying junctures, stunned into mute attention. Back to work. Drugs target receptors and transport pathways because everything is everywhere always. Chicken-chested weaklings bar access. Never again. Please hold. Another glorious display lights up the skies, but smudged pages

chastise the very thought. How will they know? I welcome their rhododendron leaves, table gifts from Shanghai, shredded documents put out to pasture. Hypothalamic controls sputter, flush with cash, and Washington fat cats soak themselves in vodka. Licensing boards diddle their time away. A nebula turns, and striations help to differentiate between system states, but it requires more. I peer out the venetian blinds at someone on a bicycle getting ready to leave for unknown parts. A famous aviatrix dies in a plane crash, even though nulliparous. I watch in horror as waves wash away house and trees along the shoreline. Mitosis takes its orders from command central. Benefits have expired. Recommendations are entertained now that divorce and poisons are in the air. They imagine all they have to do is demand, but who wants what from whom? Deadbeats expectorate, swathed in strawberry aroma and swaddling bands. Wishes are defeated, but it may not be for years. No refunds under any circumstances. Just ask that jailer if you want confirmation. Arable soil holds out hope, despite common frustrations. Nothing turns into anything else but becomes ever more itself.

224
War reverses the tide. Tiny blotches materialize and vanish, as wounds, then grave markers.

San Diego
March 3, 2010-August 3, 2010

Printed in Great Britain
by Amazon

76269913R00068